The Adventures of Anderson

Arlen Curtis Matson
Psalm 1:3

written by

Arlen Curtis Matson

Illustrations by

Tenille Enger

AuthorHouse™
1663 Liberty Drive, Suite 200
Bloomington, IN 47403
www.authorhouse.com
Phone: 1-800-839-8640

This book is a work of fiction. People, events, and situations are the product of the author's imagination. Any resemblance to actual persons, living or dead, or historical events, is purely coincidental.

First published by AuthorHouse 4/24/2008

ISBN: 978-1-4343-4682-7 (sc)

Printed in the United States of America
Bloomington, Indiana

This book is printed on acid-free paper.

Scripture quotations used in this book are taken from the Holy Bible, King James Version.

Dedicated to my dearest wife, Arlene,
adventuring with me to all of those
"pleasant places"

To all of the "young authors" from
Old Mission, Oak Park and Sabin
Elementary Schools

To our Mennonite friends Roman
and Fannie Schlabach

Table of Contents

Preface

There was a day in the Upper Peninsula of Michigan when iron mining was king. I entered into this world in 1934, born on a small farm in Bates Township a few miles north of Iron River.

Ice cream was a rare treat. Root beer in a gallon jug from the A&W was a special highlight on those hot days during the summer. It seemed as though there was always a crowd of children gathered at Forsberg's store. Penny candy was a major decision with root beer barrels, taffy suckers, and jawbreakers as some of the popular ones.

This was the end of the Depression era and pre-World War II. The CCC's and WPA were government programs providing employment for most parents unless they could exist as farmers.

Times were tough and money scarce, but creativity was at its zenith. In our community, boys and girls went to school in red and white school buses. Their milk money was tied into one corner of a handkerchief, and they never left home without one. It's strange how important the handkerchief for the boys and the hankie for the girls was esteemed.

Principals or superintendents spanked students for misbehavior, and it was done in the gym at our school. I suppose the echo in the school had an effect on the students.

The most dreaded event occurred when the siren at the nearby Rogers Mine went off. This indicated that there had been some sort of an accident or cave-in. All pencils would stop writing in the classroom as children would look up at the clock mounted to the front of the room between pictures of Washington and Lincoln. Their minds would begin the checklist of family members or relatives who were working that day. It would be a rare student who didn't have someone working in the iron ore mine.

Never did the thought of becoming a teacher enter my mind until years later. I was serving my country in the Air Force stationed in Morocco. I had recently married my high school sweetheart. We were together on this tour of duty and spent much of our two years learning about the Moroccan way of life. There were many opportunities to observe children with little schooling and the strange lack of respect they received by many adults in that culture. This was coupled with the fact that I had become a Christian during my junior year in high school. I knew that Jesus Christ was not only my Savior, but also a master teacher. This led me to pursue a career of teaching elementary students.

After thirty-two years of teaching in grades four, five, and six, a new season entered my life as I retired. All the books that I had read to my students during those years and young authors' assignments, prompted me to try writing a book. Childhood memories began flooding my mind with thoughts, and then I recalled an incident that had occurred when I was twelve. It had happened on an early spring campout with the Boy Scouts near Lake Superior. The prologue in this book is that true adventure that scared me like no other event in all of those school days.

From this incident, I began recalling other adventures in Ironwood, Michigan. The places in this book are real as well as those three friends. Although the stories are fiction, the activities engaged in are true. Welcome to the adventures of Curtis Anderson and his three friends in *The Adventures of Anderson.*

Prologue

Mr. Ekstrom, the Scoutmaster of Troop 143, announced that our spring campout would be held at an abandoned logging camp near Lake Superior. After a long, cold winter, we couldn't wait to get outside and explore the woods again. It was to be held on the third week of April during our Easter vacation from school.

We assembled into our patrols and planned for the trip. This done, my best friend, Bryce, and I planned on some personal things we would do together. Our free-time adventure was going to be fishing with homemade spears.

Bryce and I met the following Saturday at his house. Thanks to our moms, we had a collection of six four-foot-long brass curtain rods. These were the old-fashioned kind. Using his dad's grinding wheel, we sharpened the ends of the thin quarter-inch rods into deadly spears. We couldn't wait to try them out.

On a Thursday evening, seven weeks later, our Scoutmaster and seventeen Boy Scouts pulled into the old logging camp. There were two long tarpapered barracks still standing in a field of stumps and saplings. Bryce and I, along with the older Scouts, took the first barracks. The younger Scouts and the Scoutmaster went into the second. Ours didn't have a stove, but we were older and didn't mind. Besides, the Scoutmaster's son, Billy, would be with his dad.

Friday was spent working on patrol projects. After lunch we used our free time as we wished. Bryce and I found a small stream with trout and threw our spears at them until our arms ached. The brookies were just too fast. It was exciting to be out in the warm sun and enjoy the quiet woods even though there was some snow on the ground.

Later, our buddies Gordon and David joined us on our spearing adventures. We spent the rest of the day throwing our spears at trees. We were pretty successful, except it was difficult trying to pull them out.

The next morning was cold and quiet. Frost covered the ground and glistened on the saplings as the sun announced a new day. We stayed in our warm, cozy sleeping bags not wanting to get up and start breakfast. Now we missed the stove and its heat.

There was a noise on the roof like a squirrel scratching. Now it was clearly moving up the roof towards the peak. It sounded like something or someone crawling. Then it stopped.

I looked at the uncovered hole in the roof where the stovepipe used to be located. All of a sudden something was coming down. It hit the old unpainted wooden floor with a cloud of dust. It was ashes. Someone was pouring stove ashes down the hole. We were being smothered in a cloud of dust.

Quickly we jumped to our feet. Choking and yelling, I put on my shoes, grabbed a spear, and ran out through the door in my underwear, furious at whoever had made this ridiculous mess. Worst of all many of us had new sleeping bags.

Once outside, I saw three younger Scouts from the next barracks running across the field for the woods. I was joined by Bryce, Gordon, and David who followed my lead carrying spears. Right away I recognized one of the culprits.

I yelled at Billy. "What did you do that for? You ruined our new sleeping bags."

He stopped, turned around, and said, "What's it to you, showoff!"

None of us liked Billy. He was a brat. He was the Scoutmaster's son, and he got away with murder in our troop. I decided enough was enough, and I would teach him a lesson once and for all.

He was standing at the edge of the clearing about a hundred feet away and squarely facing us. Without thinking, I took the spear, reached back as far as I could, and threw it at him. I wanted to come close enough to scare some sense into his thick skull.

The brass spear sailed through the air in a huge arc gleaming like a meteor streaking towards the earth, and then fear struck my soul as I saw it embed itself into Billy's left thigh.

All of us stood there in silence waiting for him to scream. The brass spear stuck in his leg swaying back and forth. No one moved. He was frozen like a statue.

Realizing what I had done and that the spear could have just as easily gone through his heart, I ran for Billy as fast as I could. He stood there in shock, unable to move or say anything. I grabbed the spear and jerked it out from his leg.

"Pull down your pants! I've got to see if you're hurt."

In the cold morning air, I didn't consider his embarrassment. My heart was pounding as I looked and saw no blood, not even a drop. There was only a small puncture, but I knew that it had gone through to the bone, or it wouldn't have stuck in his leg.

"Bryce...quick...go back to the barracks and get the first-aid kit, soap, and water."

After cleaning the wound and covering it with a simple bandage, I said, "Is there anything more you want me to do to help you?"

He looked up into my face with his fearful eyes and replied, "Don't tell my dad. It was my fault anyway. I started it."

Billy never told his dad what happened. He had no consequences from the injury, and I became like an older brother to him. From that day on, Billy's behavior ceased from being obnoxious, and I never again threw a brass spear.

Chapter I

Two Wheels to Iron River

The early morning June sun came streaming through the yellow curtains of the bedroom window. Curtis could feel its warmth on his face. He had deliberately not pulled the shades down the night before. He wanted the sun to wake him up.

Quick as a wink, he scampered out of bed and dressed. A passing glance out the window told him all he wanted to know—no wind moving the branches and clear blue sky. The Big Ben clock hands were on five-thirty. Everything was perfect for the ninety-mile bicycle trip to Iron River.

Curtis combed his light brown hair ever so carefully, parting it on the left side. He washed the thick glasses with warm water removing all the oily smears that were a continuous problem. It was one thing to have to wear the gold-rimmed thick glasses, but quite another to have such greasy skin. He pulled his solid white sweatshirt outward trying to make his body appear wider, but the kids at school were right in calling him skinny. However, that would all change when they heard that he was the first boy to bike from Ironwood to Iron River. That would make him famous in their eyes.

"Now, Curtis, you call us from Grandma's house as soon as you get there. We'll pay for the call," his dad said. "You've done a fine job polishing your Monarch bike. I checked your valves for rim cuts, and there aren't any."

"Thanks, Dad," Curtis replied. "I really worked hard with the toothbrush and kerosene cleaning up the chain. I oiled it like you said and then wiped off all the excess so it won't pick up a lot of dirt on the trip."

The family gathered outside. The blue and ivory Monarch with its chrome fenders and shock absorbers was clean as a whistle.

"Remember now," his dad repeated, "call when you get there."

Curtis biked south from his house and turned east onto US 2. He noticed far off to the west an extremely dark bank of clouds.

I better make sure those clouds don't gain on me, or I'm going to be in trouble, he thought to himself. He increased his peddling speed.

The towns rolled by quickly. First there was Bessemer, then Ramsey, and it seemed as if in no time he was approaching Wakefield. He liked Wakefield with its tall wooden ski jump, Sunday Lake, and the high school sports emblem. The deep red cardinal was so colorful on the uniforms and the cheerleaders' sweaters.

Next stop—Marinesco, twenty miles down the road. Each town and intersection made for an accomplishment of some sort. It meant one less mile. He had already seen a doe, two fawns, a black bear, and many red-tailed hawks looking for road kill.

Two hours later, Curtis spied an A&W Root Beer stand. He pulled up to the side of the building and parked his bike. His mouth was dry. He had not stopped since he had left Ironwood and hadn't drunk a drop of water. He ordered a giant-sized, frost-covered mug of root beer. Next to a chocolate malt, this was his favorite drink.

Seated nearby were a woman and a girl of about his age. "May I ask you for the time?" he said.

The lady replied, "Nine-thirty. I noticed your beautiful bicycle when you drove up. I've never seen one with two springs on the front. It's most unusual. The color is striking. I thought all boys' bicycles were red."

Curtis smiled and set down the large frosted mug of root beer. "I worked for two years delivering newspapers in order to get that bike. My dad went in on it with me, fifty-fifty. I'm from Ironwood. I've been planning a bike trip to Iron River for a long time. I'm riding ninety miles to my grandma's house over near Iron River. I hope to be the first person to complete the trip on a bicycle."

He continued, "Since World War II is over, the bike companies have decided to paint bicycles different colors. Blue is beautiful. The two chrome springs on the front fork cushion the ride on all kinds of roads. I am very proud of my bike."

The woman and the girl got up and walked over.

Curtis rose from his stool.

"My name is Mrs. Lauti, and this is my daughter, Veronica. We live in Wakefield. We drove over to Marinesco today to visit my father."

Curtis looked at Veronica. He had never seen such deep blue eyes, and the sun seemed to strike the slight tint of auburn in her long dark brown hair. He liked her right away. Standing there captured by her eyes, he looked back to Mrs. Lauti and said, "My name is Curtis Anderson, and I'm glad to know both of you."

Veronica spoke up with a puzzled look on her face. "What are you going to do if it rains? Look at those dark clouds over there." Then she laughed. "I bet you're going to sing the song, *Singing in the Rain*...and just keep right on pedaling."

Curtis started singing the song and then said, "A singer I am, but that storm will never catch me. You see, my Monarch bike has the new speed chain, and I've been riding all over the countryside getting ready for this trip. I really believe I can outrun it."

Curtis left the root beer stand refreshed and renewed in spirit. His heart was full of joy. He was over a third of the way. He kept seeing Veronica's face in his mind as he traveled the next fifteen miles to Watersmeet. He would remember that name, Veronica Lauti.

The dark clouds from the west had gained on him as he approached Watersmeet. It was eleven o'clock, and there was still forty miles to go. He was hungry as a bear, but also a little tired. He knew that his pace was fast because he was fearful of being marooned by the storm or struck by lightning. He stopped for a hamburger, glass of water, and a Baby Ruth candy bar.

From here on the terrain of the country changed from rolling hills and flat areas to huge hills. Many of them were from a half mile to a mile long. Of course, it would be a thrilling ride down.

Curtis loved Grandma Anderson. He was looking forward to staying at the farm for most of the summer. He would go swimming, fishing, and play ball with his friend, Chester.

As he approached Sun Lake, he slowed down to observe a huge box turtle crossing the road. This was one of the things he liked about bicycling. The bike was quiet as it moved. It didn't disturb the animals. Someday he would be a forest ranger and work in the outdoors. The scenery was a continuous mix of forests, lakes, and rivers. Watersmeet also marked the location of the continental divide.

Curtis looked at the reflection of the sky in the lake. To his surprise he noticed dark clouds near the west shore. *Wow! How did they get here so fast? I've got to pick up my speed.*

For the next two hours, it was a battle against the hills. His stomach was also churning from the hastily eaten hamburger and candy bar. His legs were losing their drive to get up the next hill. He wanted to report back to his dad and friends that he had climbed every hill. Now he realized it couldn't be done.

The wind from the west had increased. His t-shirt was drenched with sweat. The dark clouds were nearly overhead. He walked up the hill with a pain in his left side.

I must be getting near Beechwood, he thought. *That means only fifteen miles to Grandma's.*

At the top of the hill, Curtis approached an intersection. His face was flushed.

I have to rest and regain my strength, he decided.

Slowly he pushed the shiny Monarch over to the intersection sign. He looked at the lettering. It read "Wisconsin...20 miles; Iron River...15 miles." He laid his bike down on the mowed grass near the sign. Using the front wheel of the bike for a headrest, he lay down and fell asleep.A terrific crack of lightning woke Curtis to a sudden cloudburst. It was difficult to see. He jumped on his bike and headed down the road. Peddling as fast as he could, he started looking for some escape from the storm. At the same time he could sense that the highway material under his tires was different from US 2. Slowly he realized that he was not heading for Iron River, but the Wisconsin border.

He saw an old barn off in a hayfield. Discovering an open gate, he headed for relief from the rain. He was soaked, but the rain had sure revived his aching body.

Opening the barn door, he pushed his two-wheeled friend into one of the stalls used for horses. His clothes were sopping wet. One by one he took them off and wrung the water out.

"There, that feels better. Good thing it's a warm rain, or I'd catch a cold for sure," he said aloud.

Curtis looked around while the rain riveted the steel corrugated roof. There were tall poles holding up the roof. He counted six stalls for horses, but the doors had been removed except for the last two. Behind him was a loft loaded with old hay. He noticed a built-in ladder leading up to a hole in the floor, and that was where he headed.

If I'm careful not to stir up too much dust, I don't think it will bother my hay fever, he thought.

Curtis was born with hay fever. He loved playing in his grandfather's red barn, but it always cost him a bout with sneezing afterwards. One time his friends had counted twelve sneezes in a row.

"I'll just lay on this soft hay and rest awhile until it stops storming," he said, and then he fell asleep.

Suddenly Curtis awoke to a new sound. It wasn't thunder or lightning this time. The rain had stopped. The night was black as soot. It sounded like a truck. Then he heard the squeak of brakes. He moved to the side of the loft and peered through a knothole in the weathered siding. There were headlights, and then there was darkness.

Both doors of an old red Chevy pickup opened, and three individuals got out. One of them was carrying a flashlight and the guy in the middle was carrying some sort of duffel bag. Curtis lay down on the hay and waited.

The huge barn door creaked on rusty hinges as they opened it. The leader began to shine the light, examining the inside. "Must be an old horse barn," he said. "See them stalls over there. They ain't got no stanchions for cows."

"We gotta hurry and hide this thing," the man with the duffel bag barked. "The further we get out of this area, the safer it will be for all of us."

"Okay, Jim. Let's find a good spot to hide the money," the man with the flashlight said. "How about in one of them stalls?"

Curtis had put his bike in the last stall. If they went over and examined the stalls, he was a dead duck. Fortunately, there was a door on the stall where he parked his wet bike.

Curtis wiggled his partially dry body to the edge of the loft. The man was shining the light at the stalls. His bike was in the furthest stall. A boy, slightly older than he was, walked over to the stall next to his bike and opened the door.

"How about under the hay in this here stall?" he asked.

"No good!" exclaimed Jim. "It's too conspicuous."

The boy closed the door and noticed water in front of the next stall. "How come there's water in front of this door and not the one I just opened?"

He was about to open the door of the last stall when Jim yelled at the kid. "Hey, Henry! See if you can pull up on that floorboard with the small hole in it over by the first stall."

As Curtis watched the young man pull up on the board, he began to wheeze. Quickly he pinched his nose just in time to prevent a sneeze. As long as he could remember, he had suffered with hay fever. First the bike scare, now his nose. His heart was thumping on the hay like a partridge drumming on a log.

Henry yanked the board up with nails attached only on the end farthest from the hole. All three fellows peered down to see a hollow area between two floor timbers deep enough to hide the duffel bag.

"This will work," said Jim. "We'll roll the duffel up and cram it down and back some behind the other floorboards. We'll come back in a few weeks when things cool down. First, let's count up the money and see what our take is "

Curtis peered through a crack between two boards in the loft watching the two men arrange the bills in different piles. The boy named Henry was holding the light.

"Hey, Jim!" said the other man wearing an old Stetson hat. "I ain't never saw so much money in all my life. Six hundred and seventeen dollars is quite a take. You sure picked that IGA store in Eagle River as a patsy. If you keep picking 'em like this, we're gonna get rich in a hurry."

Replacing the board with the hole in it, they covered it slightly with hay.

"In a couple two three weeks we'll come back and live like kings," promised Jim. "Wait here a minute. I've got to get rid of all that Coke I drank from the store and then we'll drive the back roads to Hagerman Lake and spend some time in my uncle's cabin."

Curtis watched as Jim shined the light on the door of the last stall and headed for it. As he approached it, Curtis shivered, wondering what the guys would do when they found his wet bike in it. Suddenly Jim chose the fifth stall instead, did his duty, and before Curtis knew it, the truck had started up and left him alone.

He waited in the loft trying to estimate how far the truck had gone before he decided to leave. After awhile he heard the wind kicking up. He decided to leave the money alone and head back for the main highway.

Quietly he took his bike out of the stall, sneaked out the barn door, and headed for US 2.

After a short distance, he decided it was safe to turn on his fender light. Before long he heard the traffic from the main highway. As he approached the stop sign, his light flashed on a parked vehicle with a yellow insignia on the door. It was a state police car. As he rode up, an officer got out and walked up to him.

"My name is Sergeant Renaldi. Aren't you a long ways from nowhere?"

"Yes, sir!" replied Curtis. "I'm on a bike trip to Iron River. I got lost in the rain. Are you looking for someone? I hope it's not me."

"No! It's not you. We have roadblocks set up all around this area. There was a robbery this evening in Eagle River, and we're trying to catch the crooks that stole quite a bit of money. Two of the guys have Luger pistols and are considered dangerous. They are driving an old red Chevrolet pickup."

Curtis gulped and his eyes widened. "I saw them. I know where the money is hidden." He told the officer the whole story about being tired, the storm, sleeping in the old barn, and what he saw from the loft.

And then he said, "I know where they're headed. To Hagerman Lake. And, and there are three of them. And they're driving a red Chevrolet truck. The oldest guy is called Jim, and the young kid a little older than me is Henry."

Sergeant Renaldi radioed this information to the other officers. They put the bike in the trunk of the black Ford and headed for the barn. Inside, he led the trooper to the board with the hole in it. The sergeant retrieved the duffel bag of money.

Officer Renaldi replied, "There's enough money in this bag to buy a new car. Now, I've got to go back to the stop sign and keep a lookout for that red truck. Would you like me to get someone to take you to your grandma's farm?"

"No, thanks! My goal is to be the first boy to bicycle from Ironwood to Iron River, and I'm going to keep the promise I made to my dad even if it means riding in the dark. I've got a light on my bike, and it's only fifteen miles to my grandma's place. I will take a ride back to the stop sign though."

Curtis headed east with his sturdy Monarch under a clear evening sky of stars. The moon was coming up over the tree line as he poured the coals to his pedals.

What an adventure I've had, he thought. *Wait 'til my buddies hear about this!*

Up and down the long hills he peddled. He thought about the lady and her daughter, Veronica, he had met from Wakefield.

I wonder if the robbery and my helping the state police find the money will be in the newspaper.

Every mile was a long climb followed by a super fast downhill descent. Sometimes it was so fast his bicycle would begin to shimmy, and he would have to use his coaster brake to slow down. Ahead of him was a familiar level stretch of macadam beginning with a long curve.

He knew this would put him about five miles from his destination. As he headed into the curve, a doe and fawn ran across the road in front of him onto a two- track road on his right.

"Pow!" There was a loud bang. He felt his rear tire on metal and realized what happened.

So near and yet so far, he thought, *and I don't have a pump or a patch kit.*

There had been little traffic tonight, and now he knew he would have to hitch a ride with someone. He listened for the faintest sound of an engine. And then he heard a sound coming up the two-track road he had just passed. It was moving slowly, and the beam of the headlights kept bouncing up and down on the tall spruce trees. This would be his salvation and to think he hardly had to wait for help.

The vehicle approached the highway cautiously and then turned in his direction. Curtis got as close to the wet pavement as was safe. The lights were on bright and partially blinded him, but he waved anyway. It was a red truck, and inside he could see three people.

The young boy on the right had rolled down his window and asked, "You got a problem, kid? Kind of late to be out joy riding, ain't it?"

Curtis recognized Henry, one of the robbers from the barn. What was he going to do? Quickly he realized that he knew them, but they didn't know him. He would have to be cool, calm, and collected because he knew that two of them had German Luger pistols.

"Do you need a hand?" Henry asked again.

"I just blew a tire. There's a Sinclair gas station about a mile up ahead, and I'm quite sure they can fix it if they're still open. I think they close at eleven o'clock."

The driver yelled across his two buddies. "Hey, kid! Thanks for the tip. We're about out of gas. Get in the back with your bike. We'll give you a lift."

Curtis was in a dilemma. *I better do as they say, or they may get suspicious.*

At the gas station the truck pulled up to the pumps. There was only one young man on duty. The driver said,

"Fill her up!"

The other two guys got out of the truck and went into the station to wait.

Curtis got down from the Chevy truck that was missing its tailgate. He went inside to wait his turn and figure out a way to be safe. He saw the restroom signs and quickly went into the Men's Room and locked the door. Immediately, he realized that he should have taken his bike off from the truck first.

He listened to the voices of Henry and the other guy. There was the ring of the cash register being opened, and a whispered comment, "Stuff your pockets with all the bills you can."

Then silence.

A few minutes later he heard the squeal of tires and someone shouting, "Hey, come back here!"

Curtis thought of his bike in the back of the truck. He ran out of the station to see the red truck speeding down the road. On the road lay his beautiful blue and ivory Monarch bicycle. Because he hadn't been in the truck to hold it, it had slid off onto the road.

The service station keeper yelled, "They didn't pay me for the gas! They just high tailed it. I'm gonna call the police."

Curtis ran down the road towards his bike. It lay on its side with two bent rims, handlebars cockeyed, and a pedal snapped off. He examined it closer. The crank was missing some teeth, and the shinny chrome headlight lay beside the edge of the road.

For nearly two years Curtis had saved his money by delivering two different newspapers, one in the morning and the other in the evening. And now he had nothing but a heap of junk. He was heart sickened. He picked up the bike and walked back to the gas station. With one more trip, he brought back the pieces.

The station attendant came running out. "I called the sheriff and told him what happened. They told me those guys are wanted for armed robbery. They took all of the cash in my register and helped themselves to a bunch of candy bars."

Curtis retold the story of his scare in the old barn and his historical bicycle trip from Ironwood to Iron River. He even told the lanky, freckled-face attendant about delivering newspapers.

"Hey! My name is Luba. I'm mostly a grease monkey around here, and I work nights to pay for my spiffy new Jeepster. I keep an old bike in the back of the garage just for little errands. How'd you like to borrow it and finish your trip?"

Curtis wiped his wet eyes and smiled a smile a mile wide.

Into the driveway came a red flashing state police car with its siren whining. Out jumped Sergeant Renaldi. "Hey, Curtis! What are you doing here? Are you planning to be a detective when you grow up?"

Then the tall trooper looked down at the boy's feet and saw his mangled bicycle. "I think you have another story to tell me. I'm sorry to see that beautiful machine come to such a sad end."

Curtis and Luba both gave their account of the scare they had at the Sinclair Gas Station. Trooper Renaldi offered to give Curtis a ride home, but he declined. He did take him up on his offer to call his parents, since it was getting so late.

It was now nearly ten o'clock as Curtis mounted the red and white Montgomery Ward bicycle and headed the remaining five miles to his grandmother's farm. He knew she would be worried; nevertheless, he appreciated her patience towards him on many occasions before. He knew she would be understanding.

About an hour before midnight, Curtis completed his long excursion that had begun at six o'clock that morning. Grandma

Anderson was happy to see him. He sat down to all the food he could eat. He was famished. He ate a loaf of toasted bread cut up into small pieces and mixed up into a bowl with a half dozen soft-boiled eggs. This was one of his favorite meals. He drank a couple quarts of milk. He ate and ate and ate and talked and talked to his beloved grandma Anderson.

As the old marble clock on the mahogany mantle struck twelve, he gave her a good night hug and headed upstairs.

There were four bedrooms upstairs, and each one was painted a different color. His favorite was the green room. He lay down on top of the bed and never heard another sound until noon the next day.

As summer vacation came to a close, Curtis gathered together all his personal things, waved down the Greyhound Bus on US 2 in front of the farm, and headed home to Ironwood. The seventh grade was coming up. He was looking forward to listening to the adventures of his three friends, Bryce, Gordon, and David. He couldn't wait to show them the clipping from the *Ironwood Daily Globe* about being the first boy to bicycle the ninety miles from Ironwood to Iron River. And then there was the other clipping: "Boy on a Bicycle Helps Recover Stolen Money."

In the second week of October, Miss Olson, the principal of Roosevelt School, called an assembly for all the students in kindergarten through eighth grade. Curtis sat next to his three close friends, Bryce, Gordon, and David. Mrs. Olson walked forward on the gym floor along with a state policeman. Curtis squinted through the thick lenses of his steel-rimmed glasses not believing what he saw. It was Sergeant Renaldi of the Michigan State Police.

What is this all about? he wondered, and he began to get nervous.

"Boys and girls, it is my honor and privilege to present today a special tribute and award to one of our students. This summer while you were on vacation, one of our seventh graders helped the state police recover over six hundred dollars that was stolen by three robbers. Not only did he show the police where the money was located, but he also identified the two men and a boy involved in the robbery. They were arrested at Hagerman Lake thanks to the information he had heard about while hiding in a barn in which the money was hidden.

"I would like Curtis Anderson to come forward and receive the school's Citizenship Certificate of Honor."

As all eyes turned towards Curtis, he adjusted his thick gold-rimmed glasses and smiled. He was a hero. This would go a long way toward removing the negative reputation he had acquired in the fourth and fifth grade.

Miss Olson continued after the long applause. "The state trooper who was involved with Curtis would also like to make a presentation."

"When my state trooper friends heard about this incident, we decided to take up a collection for a new bicycle. The store owner at Eagle River did the same with his customers. It was a sad experience to see your splendid Monarch bicycle all smashed up, especially after all your hard work to buy it. With your good deeds in helping us apprehend the crooks, many of us felt that we had to help you get another one."

Suddenly the students in the bleachers looked towards the hallway door. In walked Luba, the gas station guy, pushing a brand new blue and ivory Monarch bicycle. It was just like the original that Curtis owned.

"Hi, Curtis. Remember me. This is for you. You sure deserve it."

Miss Olson spoke up, "Most of you are aware that our school sponsors Boy Scout Troop 143. Curtis is a member of that troop. The Boy Scouts have a vow that they recite at each meeting. It is intended to be the code they live by.

It says, 'On my honor, I will do my best to do my duty to God and my country, and to obey the Scout law. To help other people at all times. To keep myself physically strong, mentally awake, and morally straight.'

"I personally want to recognize and thank Curtis Anderson for demonstrating to us the truth of this pledge in his life. He rode a one-speed bicycle ninety miles, was alert to many dangers he faced on the highway, and honored the law of the land with his honesty. It is our hope that all of you students at this assembly will live by this same code of conduct."

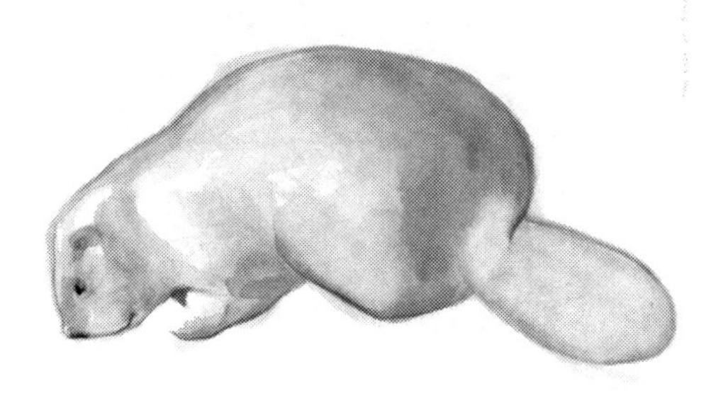

Chapter II

The Raft of Spring Creek

Curtis Anderson looked down at the shiny silver shock absorbers of his new bike as they sprung up and down on the uneven road. The memory of the adventures he had had with his first Monarch was vivid in his mind. He was proud of the blue and ivory colored Monarch with its speed chain, chrome fenders, and headlight.

He would never forget the day his dad had called from the office and told him he could pick up the bicycle after school at Peterson's Hardware Store. There were no bicycles manufactured during World War II.

When the owner of the store wheeled it out from the backroom, he said, "You have the first new bike in town since the war ended. Congratulations!"

Two years earlier Curtis had made a fifty-fifty agreement with his dad towards a new bike. For a year and a half, he had saved his money by delivering newspapers Sunday mornings and weekdays after school.

Curtis had moved to the town of Ironwood in the fourth grade. This was his seventh school, and he had made a mess of things by stealing a rusty old flat-tired three-speed bicycle from a garage. He just figured no one would miss it, and he could have fun fixing it up. A few months later, after being invited by Kenny to his birthday party, he had stolen again. This time it was Kenny's new BB pistol. It was stupid.

Curtis didn't have some of the special things most kids owned. He had fallen into the trap of coveting, and this had led him to stealing. After being confronted by the principal, he confessed. The problem was that the kids at school knew about it, and his name was mud. He was shunned by his classmates, but inside his mind he knew he wasn't all that bad.

He had a long talk with his dad about good and evil, and which force was going to be the stronger in his life. Curtis resolved to prove to the students of Roosevelt School, his family, and Grandma Anderson that he was not an evil person. The bicycle trip to Iron River proved that he had the perseverance to train and the courage to attempt a solo trip never completed by any boy before. Even though the bicycle had been destroyed near the end of the trip, his honesty had been rewarded with another identical new one. The assembly before his classmates had built up his confidence and provided an opportunity to begin building a new reputation.

For over two years he didn't have a friend until one day a new boy transferred in from another school. His name was Bryce. That fall they joined the Boy Scouts and became friends with Gordon and David. All four were also starters on the six-man football team.

Curtis was tall and skinny. His clothes hung on him like a scarecrow. With his wire-rimmed glasses that looked like two magnifying glasses wired together, he was not at all happy with his appearance. To make up for this, he combed his thick, golden brown hair immaculately. With a perfect part on the left side and a large wave in the front, it drew attention away from his grotesque appearance.

Bryce was sitting on his old green and white bike balancing himself with one foot on the front step of his house as Curtis rode up.

"Can you bring your stuff for the raft?" Curtis pushed his glasses up higher on the bridge of his nose. Oily skin and glasses were never-ending problems.

"Yup!" smiled Bryce. "I got the buck saw, some short pine boards, nails, and a hatchet. My dad said he would drop them off at Spring Creek this afternoon."

Curtis enjoyed his best friend with his blonde hair so neatly combed back. In fact, every time he saw him, it looked as though he had just come up out of a swimming pool. Bryce was a fantastic swimmer.

As they headed for school, Curtis thought that he liked his best friend most because he accepted him at face value. He didn't hold his past against him.

Gordon and David were waiting at the bike rack as they drove up to Roosevelt School. It was early, and no one was around to interrupt or spy on their secret planning session. Today was one of the most special days of the year. It was the last day of school before summer vacation and a half day at that. The big event was that he and his best friends, Bryce, Gordon, and David were going to build a raft on Spring Creek. They had been planning on this all winter.

Curtis took the little red-spiraled notebook out from his pocket as the four of them sat on a small concrete wall, which extended out from the entrance of the school.

He read off each boy's name and a list of items they were to provide for their venture.

Gordon piped up, "I can't bring my dad's draw shave, but he said it was okay to use his hatchet."

Gordon ran his right hand through his greasy, blonde crew cut causing it to bristle up like a porcupine. Of the four of them, he was the girls' favorite. Not only was he good looking with those brilliant green eyes, but he was also highly admired in the classroom because he was so smart.

"We need the draw shave for cleaning the bark off from the logs," Curtis remarked.

"We've got several at home, Curtis. I'll just bring one for each of us when we go to the creek this afternoon," answered Bryce.

"Hey, Curtis! Did your mom make our special pirate's flag?" asked David.

"She sure did! Wait till' you see it. It's a beaut, but not until we have the raft all built. I also got a couple of screw eyes and a small rope for hoisting up our Jolly Roger onto a flagpole.

"Did everyone get permission from their parents for our summer raft project?" questioned Curtis.

"My mom and dad really thought it was a neat idea, thanks to you," said Bryce. "They gave me strict orders that we should always remain in sight of the highway once we got to sailing our rig."

The north-south highway extended up a long hill and could be seen for miles around from Spring Creek. Both of the other boys agreed. They could raft on the creek, but had to stay within sight of the road. Their parents didn't want them getting lost.

The school bell rang, and Curtis reminded everyone to bring their snacks and pocket knives.

As Curtis made his way down the crowded hall to his locker, he accidentally bumped into Kenny. He apologized, but the doctor's son just kept on walking away from him without a word of reply. Ever since Curtis had swiped his BB pistol in the fourth grade, Kenny had always kept his distance.

For two years, after having apologized to Kenny and his parents, Curtis had had an uphill battle to prove he wasn't a bad kid. Even though he had stolen a bike and a gun, he only had three friends who accepted him. Gordon and David were also new students. Somehow he had to prove to this school that he could be one of their leaders. Instead, he had been considered a sissy because he wouldn't fight when the other boys would tease him. Of course, he was afraid too. One more incident would be "strike three," and he would be expelled from school.

About two o'clock that Friday afternoon, the four boys having successfully passed into the next grade, began sawing and hauling dead dry cedar logs to the edge of Spring Creek. Each was to be twelve feet long and at least eight inches in diameter. Bryce and David sawed the logs to length, and Gordon and Curtis towed them to a slight incline near the creek. They began laying them out side by side so they would fit together with the fewest gaps.

Bryce came up to Curtis and said, "I think we should strip off the bark before lashing them together, or we're going to be slipping all over the place once they get wet. I'll get the draw shaves."

"Great thinking!" exclaimed Curtis. "Let's look at our drawing and see if there's anything else we should do before putting this contraption together."

All four boys agreed. They would start lashing as soon as the bark was off and remove any knobs that might prevent a good fit.

Three hours went by as they completed the second phase of the project. They began lashing. Working in teams of two, they took the sisal rope and started weaving it between each log.

Gordon's green eyes gleamed. "Boy, would Mrs. Solon be thrilled to see her art students using the placemat skills we learned in that weaving unit."

As they reached the halfway point, David took a deep breath, bulging out his muscular chest. "How are we going to make the observation hole?"

Curtis replied, "Let's cut the logs now before we go any further. Remember, our plan calls for a square foot hole in the middle of the raft."

This they did and completed the rest of the lashings. Tired, but satisfied with their progress, they all jumped into the creek and had a mud-slinging water fight.

A short time later, the quartet sat on the small bank admiring the slow shallow meandering stream flowing under a cloudless canopy of blue space. They were drawn to the sight of the rough-hewn raft by the aroma of freshly cut cedar logs. The day was creeping near suppertime.

Curtis jumped up, having just cleaned his thick spectacles and said, "Let's head for home. We've got all day tomorrow to finish this job."

Early the next morning, the four boys raced to Spring Creek. David was the first one to arrive on his red and white Columbia bicycle. "Hey! Look at those muddy raccoon tracks all over our raft."

Curtis took a wrinkled plan from his shirt pocket and said to the group, "David, why don't you and Bryce work on the observation box. Gordon and I will get the mast ready. Whoever gets done first can begin cutting the crosspieces that will bind the raft together in case the lashings ever break."

By noon, the four-foot-tall observation box had been nailed into place, and the mast had been anchored behind the box. The mast was a thin aspen sapling about nine feet tall and cleanly shaven.

"Hey, guys," said Curtis, "look at this monstrosity we've built. The mast even has a screw eye for the rope when we hoist up the flag."

"That's one Noah's Ark. How are we ever going to get the rope through that screw eye now that it's way up in the air?" inquired David.

"Good question." Curtis smiled in his usual confident manner. "We'll figure that one out later when we begin our maiden voyage."

"What shall we christen this thing?" queried Gordon.

"How about the Ark of Spring Creek," volunteered David.

Everyone agreed unanimously.

They enjoyed a leisurely lunch and the quiet spaciousness of this pleasant place. The afternoon was devoted to cutting, hewing, and carefully shaping two poling poles and two paddles.

After a day of rest on Sunday, the foursome arrived the next day on their bikes in a dead heat. As they braked simultaneously with their coaster brakes, the noise flushed a pair of redhead ducks swimming near their prize hand-crafted ark.

Bryce had a puzzled look on his face and spoke up first. "How are we ever going to get this colossal thing into the water?"

"That's simple," replied Curtis. "We're going to tie a rope to the front of it and stretch it across the creek to that big maple. You and I can pull on the rope. David and Gordon will take the two poles and lever it from behind. Any other questions?"

Everyone yelled, "Let's go for it!"

An hour later, the four laborers had moved the raft barely a yard. "This will never do!" groaned David. His black hair and tan muscular back glistened with sweat. "We got to do better than this. Come on, Gordon, give us another history lesson."

Bryce lifted his mucky, sulfur-smelling feet up onto the bank and said, "Let's take a break. We need to think this one over."

A long silence followed with heavy breathing.

Gordon brushed his porky crew cut back and spoke up. Though he was small and somewhat frail for his age, he made up for it with his agility and amazing memory. No wonder he was the quarterback of their six-man football team.

"Do any of you remember what we learned about in social studies when we were studying the Middle Ages? They had a similar problem. Once they got the sieging tower built out of heavy logs, how did they move it to the castle wall?"

Quick as a wink, Curtis yelled, "That's it! It'll work! I know it will! Thanks, Gordon. You're a genius. Let's cut some logs for rollers."

They cut eight more logs and placed five of them under the raft. The extra three were placed in front. Now, with two of them pulling on the rope and two levering from the rear, the raft slowly moved onto the extra logs. Once the raft was on the three front logs, they would stop and bring the freed logs from behind the raft. Since they had built the raft on a slight incline, it didn't take a great deal of effort to move it forward.

Finally, it rolled into the water. It looked like a battleship in the small creek and barely had enough water to float.

Curtis ran to his pack and pulled out the rolled-up pirate's flag. Quickly he ran back to the bank and leaped onto the raft. Curtis was the best leaper in school, thanks to his ski-jumping ability. He was always jumping. In fact, whenever he ran, he continuously jumped with every fifth or sixth step. Some of the kids even called him "Kangaroo."

Curtis unfurled the white flag. There was a black skull-and-crossbones design stitched in the middle of both sides. In the corners appeared the initials of each boy: B, C, D, and G. They were done in each boy's favorite color. Everyone admired Curtis' mother's handiwork.

"Hey, Curtis!" exclaimed Gordon. "Have you figured out how to get the rope for the flag through the screw eye way up there on the mast?"

"Yup! First let me thread this rope through the sleeve in the flag. Gordon, you stand on David's shoulders and string it through the screw eye. Bryce and I will balance you two."

Once this was done, Curtis gave the command, *"Pre...sent arms!"*

They all saluted the waving flag together. The raft of Spring Creek was now commissioned for sailing and poling adventures for the rest of summer.

During the ensuing weeks, the same quartet of bicycles could be seen racing back and forth down the macadam highway to Spring Creek. Even a curious red fox became a fixture of the scene perching itself every morning on a nearby grassy knoll.

The kinship of the four fellows grew as they would play John Paul Jones, broad jump off the raft into the cool shallow water, and fish for shiners. Most of all they took turns peering down the observation box. By placing a canvas over the box and crawling inside, they were able to look down the small wooden shaft and observe a whole new world of aquatic life. There were crayfish, shiners, turtles, frogs, snakes, colorful rocks, a little muskrat, sometimes a trout, and even an old wagon wheel.

One day in mid-August, three of the boys were sunning themselves on the bank when David announced from the raft, "I saw the coach yesterday, and he mentioned that football practice starts next week."

"I know," said Curtis as he got up and strolled into the water. "Summer's almost over, and school will be here before you know it. I've been thinking about having a special celebration before we go back. What would you all think about having an exploration trip? We could float down the creek like 'Minn of the Mississippi.' The water is so shallow here that it's not much fun anymore."

"How far are you thinking of going?" queried Bryce. "Remember, we promised our folks that we would always stay within sight of the main road."

Curtis stepped from the shallow stream up onto the cedar raft. "I know, but if you look at the road from the lay of the land, you can see we're in a valley. We can see cars and trucks going up that road for miles around."

"With all the logjams downstream, I don't think we'll get very far in a week anyway," responded Gordon.

"What do you say, guys?" challenged Curtis. "It would be a great way to build up our muscles for football. We've still got our tools hidden under that old barn door we found laying on the ground where we built the raft."

They all consented, but with the understanding that they would honor the agreement with their parents.

The next four days were spent sawing and chopping gateways through the water barricades big enough for the large five-by-twelve-foot raft to navigate.

By early Thursday afternoon, they came upon a huge logjam. A large deep pond had formed, and to their delight beavers were swimming back and forth carrying branches with leaves on them. Curtis had also noticed that the banks of Spring Creek were getting steeper. There was a brook flowing into the pond above the dam.

"Wow! This is about the size of Ramsey Park," observed Gordon.

"Hey, David! Why don't you climb the bank above that little stream and find out if you can still see the highway?" suggested Curtis.

With a wrinkled forehead Gordon spoke slowly. "We'll never be able to cut out this massive logjam. I know of no way."

"I think we've gone far enough anyway," cautioned Bryce.

While the three boys stood intrigued by the swimming of the beavers, David yelled back from the top of the hill. "Come on up and see this view. It's fantastic!"

All three boys scurried up the steep ravine and looked upon miles of forests, deep valleys, and the pond beneath them. Their silver stream meandered westward unobstructed as far as they could see. Then a sharp bend obstructed the view from its mysterious destination.

"Wow! Would it ever be daring to ride beyond this barricade." Gordon was excited just as he was before a football game. "We'd be free as a bird. No more cutting logs and blistered hands."

"From here on there's no way you can see the road," said Bryce. "My parents would probably take away my football season if we did. I want to play right end again and catch more passes than last year."

"Mine too!" agreed Curtis. I love playing left halfback. We wouldn't have much of a six-man football team if the four of us were missing."

Curtis shivered without his shirt on and pointed northward. "I got a feeling that cold wind is coming off from Lake Superior. I don't think we're too far away. Doesn't that sound like the crashing of waves?"

They decided to leave the tools at the big logjam, head back upstream, and then home. Tomorrow would be the big voyage down Spring Creek to this last colossus of a logjam. They all agreed to inform their parents about what they were going to do on Friday and make sure they had their blessing.

Wanting to take advantage of this special day, they all arrived early after a flying pedal to their secret spot. Quickly they jumped aboard making sure they had their paddles, poles, a canvas for the sail, extra rope, and lunches.

"Anchor's away!" shouted David as they began poling and paddling in earnest through the shallow water. It was too shallow. The morning hours found them pulling with ropes and pushing their slow-moving freighter downstream.

By late morning, the wind had picked up speed from the northeast. This gave them a little push in the back. Curtis, the weatherman of the bunch, noticed this first and motioned for the guys to take a break.

"I've got an idea. Why don't we hook up the canvas to the mast and use it as a sail to help pull us along. The water is deeper here. Bryce and David can work the sail, and Gordon and I can pole."

Together they fashioned a sailing rig. Everything worked to perfection. With the canvas billowing full of wind, they reached the last beaver pond barricade with the sun directly overhead.

"Let's feast on our mother's preparations for our celebration," exclaimed Curtis as he wiped his thick glasses with a red bandanna.

Each one took out his contribution for the special lunch they had agreed on the day before: Ritz crackers with pineapple cheese spread, ham sandwiches, Baby Ruth candy bars, Orange Crush pop, and homemade apple pie made by Bryce's mom.

It was David's turn this time to give the special pop command that Curtis had made up as the Boy Scout Troop 143 Musician. Curtis had joined the troop later in the school year. All the extra jobs that were awarded patches had no longer been available. The only job left was Troop Musician. Most guys considered singing sissy stuff. The patch to be worn on the uniform was a large embroidered harp. It was beautiful.

He was to be the leader in the troop cheers and songs. He loved music, played the saxophone, and was creative with words. Always he had ideas. Maybe it was because he was so quiet, afraid that if he raised his hand in class, he would be teased and embarrassed.

"Ready...draw...shake...open...fire!" yelled David. Each boy took out his Boy Scout knife and opened the bottle opener blade, shook the glass bottle vigorously, extracted the cap, and squirted it at each other.

Lunch concluded by eating the freshly baked apple pie and downing it with the last drop of pop. They all sat lounging on the wet orange-smelling sun-bleached logs of their fifth friend. The white flag with the black satin skull and crossbones was streaming straight out to the southwest in the strong wind. Even the initials of the boys were brilliant in the sun. It was a happy, yet melancholy moment.

"What are we going to do with the flag now that our excursion is over?" asked David.

"We could just leave it here on the pole until next summer," said Curtis.

"I've got an idea," replied Gordon.

"Oh, no!" exclaimed Bryce, "not another history lesson."

"That's what it is," laughed Gordon. "Have you ever heard of a time capsule?"

"Chalk another tally mark up for Gordon," responded Curtis.

Gordon continued, "We can find a hollow log, roll up the flag in the wax paper we used for our sandwiches. Then we'll seal the ends of the log with clay and hide it."

"That's a great idea," said Curtis, "but before we do that, I have another one. Since it's so early in the afternoon and we don't have anything else to do, what do you say we open up this last logjam for next year?

"You know, guys," spoke Curtis not looking up from the water for a tear of happiness was forming ever so slowly, "I've had one special summer. With all the trouble I've had in school the last few years, and then my grandfather dying last spring, this has been the greatest summer ever. You've all helped my hurt. You've also given me a chance to lead in things. At school, Kenny prevents me from leading in any games. He tells the kids that my judgment can't be trusted on committees. He even told Paula, our class president, that I was an evil person. Thanks a million for accepting me as I really am and being my friends."

"We're all for one and one for all," shouted Bryce encouragingly. "Let's do it, musketeers."

Wiping tears from his eyes, Curtis responded. Raising his arm in a mock sword salute, he yelled, "Let's invade the last log fortress!"

"Wait just a minute!" cautioned Bryce. "This is one big logjam, and there is a ton of water behind it. I remember my grandfather telling us stories about logging when he was a young man. He and another older fellow had just one job, removing logs that were jammed. They had a special way of releasing the logs, besides using dynamite.

Have you ever heard of a *key* log?"

Gordon laughed. "You mean your grandpa carried a special key in his pocket, and all he had to do was put it into the log and unlock it."

"Not exactly," said Bryce, "but if you come around to the back side of the logjam, I think I can show you."

The foursome climbed over the tangled web of logs and driftwood following Bryce into the water beneath the dam.

"You see where the water is roiling out from under that center section. My grandpa said that there were usually three or four logs that get caught crossways.

This prevents the whole thing from releasing. His job was to cut them out, and 'bingo' the whole jam would go."

The boys became lumberjacks and started looking for the key logs. Upon finding four that seemed to be holding the jam, they began the laborious job of sawing and prying.

Curtis took charge again and said, "This pile must be twelve feet tall; and if it ever goes, we'll have to scramble like squirrels to keep from getting crushed."

The raft, which had not been tied up, was floating freely in the water close to the logjam. The boys could hear the Jolly Roger flag flapping in the brisk wind.

Three of the four logs were sawed twice through and thrown downstream. Now there was a hole about the size of a driveway culvert, and water was gushing out.

Curtis and Bryce took the rope and tied it with a good timber hitch to the fourth key log. They stretched it out to a mature white birch tree that was leaning out into the creek. All four of them began pulling on the rope as they had when they had first launched the raft. Nothing happened.

Curtis went up and got a pole from the raft. He carefully climbed down to the taught rope. He placed the pole as a pry behind the last key log. He could see it was barely wedged behind another log. He yelled above the squirting water, "When I say now, pull with all your might."

Slowly he began to pry the jammed end upward. He got a whiff of the old green algae slime as pieces were scraped free from years of growth.

"Now!"

Suddenly everything let loose. Quick as a wink Curtis jumped for dear life towards shore. The other three had been pulling from the east bank. They stood and stared as nearly half of the logjam released itself. The whole pond was about to empty through the large gap opened by the release of the fourth key log.

"Oh, no! Here comes the raft," shouted David.

"Cut the rope from the tree, and tie it to the raft before we lose it!" yelled Curtis from the other side of the creek.

All four boys ran and swam towards the raft, which was moving quickly downstream. Bryce, the super swimmer, caught up to the raft, climbed aboard with the end of the rope in his hand. He secured it around the observation box. The other three boys grabbed the trailing rope, which was still attached to the fourth key log. Finally they all crawled on board.

"What are we going to do now?" asked David.

"We've got to get to shore. Grab the pole and paddles and let's make a beeline for the north bank," commanded Curtis.

"I can barely touch bottom with my pole," reported Gordon.

"Let's use the pole and paddles as best we can," said Curtis.

Slowly the raft began moving towards the shoreline. They were also approaching the first bend in the creek that they had seen earlier from the top of the ravine.

"David, you get the end of the rope and prepare to jump as soon as we get near enough to that bend."

Curtis removed the fourth key log and handed him the rope. As the raft caught a stronger current near the bend in the stream, all four boys stared in disbelief at what they could now see around the bend in the creek. Before their eyes, moved a large river with white water rapids created by innumerable iron-stained boulders. The splashing sounds reverberating from the canyon's walls were deafening. They were terrified.

"We must have come plumb out to the Montreal River," shouted Curtis. "Paddle for dear life. We've got to get closer to that point before we get caught in the current of the river.

"You take the paddle, Gordon, and I'll use the pole up front to steady the raft when David jumps."

David held the end of the rope in his left hand. As they neared the bend entering into the raging river, he took a running leap and landed squarely on shore. When his wet tennis shoes landed on the soft moist clay, he slipped backwards into the stream. The speed of the raft jerked the rope out of his hand. He quickly scrambled safely back onto the bank.

The raft was pulled into the current of the frothing river. The lashed logs began to take a beating as they continuously slammed into submerged and exposed boulders. The raft swung sideways out of control.

Curtis, his tanned forehead wrinkled with worry, ordered Bryce and Gordon to use their paddles to keep the raft moving lengthwise with the current.

Bryce yelled back, "Isn't there a huge falls on the Montreal River?"

"There sure is!" responded Curtis. "I've been there with my folks when we drove out to Little Girl's Point on Lake Superior."

"Do you think it's above or below us?" shouted Gordon.

Without warning, the raft stopped dead in its tracks. All three boys were thrown forward. Bryce and Gordon grabbed hold of the observation box. Curtis was hurled partially into the water, but was still holding onto his pole. Fortunately, this had become lodged in a crack between two logs at the end of the raft.

After some quick rescue work by his buddies, Gordon asked Curtis, "Where's your glasses?"

"The pole must have knocked them off when we got hung up."

"What are you going to do now?" Gordon shivered as he looked at his lanky friend. "How can you see?"

"Well, at least we're safe for the time being, but we sure are marooned. We must be hung up on a rock ledge of some sort. As for my glasses, I don't play football and basketball with them anyway. I use my instincts when I can't see clearly."

"If only we were closer to shore," said Bryce. "I could take a rope and swim for it."

"I wonder if we can play hopscotch with all those boulders sticking out of the water," suggested Curtis. "There are so many, this place looks like a checkerboard. If one of us takes the rope, swims to the next boulder downstream, encircles the rock with the rope, we could make it all the way to the riverbank."

"Bryce, since you're the best swimmer, do you think you could do it? Gordon and I can hold onto the rope and bring you back if you miss the rock."

"I'm game. We can't stay here forever. Besides it's getting near suppertime, and I'm cold. Heaven help me if my dad ever hears about this caper."

The boys pulled in the long waterlogged rope that had been trailing behind the raft. Bryce tied it around his chest. He eased into the swirling water from the downstream section of the raft. Between swimming and riding the current, he made it successfully to the first rock.

He climbed onto the large granite, removed the rope, and yelled back, "Give me some slack, and I'll loop it around the boulder and set up for the next one."

Curtis shouted back above the constant turbulence of the rapids. "Wait until Gordon and I get over to where you are before you try again. Double the rope around the rock just in case it floats up."

Gordon slid himself into the water holding tightly onto his lifeline. Suddenly, with the loss of his weight from the raft, it began to float downstream again. Curtis jumped into the water holding the remaining rope in his hands. Quickly he twisted it around his wrists.

In seconds both of them were carried below Bryce's location. Slowly they worked their way up into an eddy next to Bryce.

Gordon was able to climb onto the boulder with Bryce. The rock was too small for three of them. Curtis held onto Gordon's ankles. Bryce took the end of the rope, tied himself up, and eased back into the copper-colored water. Curtis climbed onto the wet granite and sat resting beside Gordon.

Bryce drifted downstream again, swam to the next large boulder, and anchored the rope. He yelled back above the hissing, splashing sound of the Montreal River. "Thank God for this rope. It's our lifeline."

It worked again, and they all began to take heart.

Little by little they used this method to hopscotch from one boulder to another. They also discovered that the double loop worked so well that only one person was required to help Bryce. Curtis would act as a spotter by standing up and giving instructions. Once Bryce was anchored at the next location, Curtis and Gordon would take the rope and swing in a big arc beneath their blonde-haired friend. Bryce would slowly haul them up into the safety of the next eddy. If it hadn't been so cold and dangerous, it would have been fun.

Finally, the swift current subsided. They found themselves holding onto a deadfall at the base of a steep bank. It was solid clay, and rivulets were oozing out all over.

"Are we ever going to get out of this mess?" exclaimed Gordon.

Just then they heard David's voice at the crest of the bank.

"Are you all okay down there? I've been watching you ever since I fell and lost the rope."

Curtis spotted David and yelled back. "We're freezing and weak. There is no way we can crawl up this squishy slippery clay bank."

"Tie a weight to the rope and throw it up as far as you can," responded David. "I should be able to reach it with a forked stick. I'll tie the end to a tree, and you can take turns climbing up."

One by one the threesome took turns and made it up into the friendly grasp of David's hand. They all gave him a big smile and their usual punch on the upper arm as their way of saying thank you.

After a short rest in the sun overlooking the rampaging river, they climbed up to the summit of a tree-covered bluff. Looking down, they could hear voices.

Gordon gasped, "Well, would you believe that!"

There at the bottom of the hill was a large parking lot with people walking back and forth from some kind of platform. The boys ran down exuberant at seeing civilization again. They headed for a cluster of spectators. Simultaneously they stopped and stared at a large black-stained sign. Inscribed in brilliant orange letters they read, *Montreal Falls Overlook*.

"Wow! Were we lucky!" whispered David.

"Thank God!" breathed out Bryce.

"Holy mackerel." Gordon brushed back his crew cut.

"We were above the falls!"

Slowly they climbed the steps with their muddy shoes and waterlogged clothes. They moved out to the railing on the platform.

"Look, Mommy! A raft is coming," said a little red-haired girl in a wheelchair.

"That's our raft!" exclaimed Curtis. "We just got off it about an hour ago."

Those gathered on the platform looked at the four shivering boys and then back to the raft. As it approached the falls, the crowd became deathly silent. The raft hung on the brink of the waterfalls for a moment as the Jolly Roger flag caught the red rays of the setting sun. Then the raft of Spring Creek plummeted down into a black frothy pool.

The eyes of the onlookers turned and stared at the four wide-eyed boys from Roosevelt School.

Simultaneously all three boys put their arms around Curtis, and Bryce said, "This is our leader.

Then all four boys raised their hands in the air and shouted, "We're all for one and one for all!"

Chapter III

Blind on a Hill

"What a great jump, Curtis!" yelled Bryce. "It measures nearly fifty feet. Last year you were only hitting in the mid forties."

Curtis and his three friends had been building homemade ski jumps since the beginning of Christmas vacation. This latest jump was their largest. They had found a huge rocky bluff with a natural hollow basin curving into a rise at its base. A small homemade platform at the top and some packed snow for the jump would make it complete.

The first thing they did was to sidestep (pank) with their skis on up to the top of the bluff. This would compact the fluffy snow for a smooth approach to the jump. All four boys then took their snow shovels and made a large mound of snow for the takeoff platform.

"Gordon, why don't you start sidestepping (panking) up the takeoff mound while I sculpture and pack the sides? When you get the top done, let me know if you have a clear view of the whole jump."

A short time later Gordon commented to Curtis, "It's a great view, but I'm not going down until I see someone else do it first."

"Don't worry. I'll lay down the first track," replied Curtis.

Bryce and David had gone down beyond the jump to the landing slope. They were packing it by repeatedly panking up and down the lower hill. A well-packed landing meant the snow would support the jumpers when they landed.

"What a gorgeous day to ski jump." Curtis made his way up the platform. "Look at that blue sky and those millions of trees all around us. What a view. I love to ski jump. You can see so much of the world when you're high on a hill."

"How far do you think we can jump from our new hill?" asked Gordon.

"My guess is we'll hit fifty feet with no trouble at all. I'm just going to let my skis take me down the first time and set a straight track.

"How do you like your new hickory skis?" asked Curtis.

"They're really solid when I land," said Gordon. "There's no chatter, and the extra weight gives me more control."

"I'd sure like a pair of jumping skis," Curtis sighed. "I've heard that the three grooves on the bottom were really designed to hold the skis straight. The extra length sure makes them heavy. I think it acts something like an anchor and keeps gravity pulling you in the right direction."

The two boys working at the bottom of the hill yelled, "We're done! Give it a try."

Curtis stepped into his toe plate and pulled the spring cable up onto the groove in the heel of his old brown leather ski boots. Once this was done, he pushed the lever in front of each shoe firmly down with a metallic snap onto wood. This was all that held him on the skis as he soared through the air. He double-checked the steel bindings making sure his boots were secure.

"Hey, Gordon! Remember when we used inner tube rubbers to hold our skis on? This must be my sixth year ski jumping."

"And what about those canning jar rubbers we used?" Gordon laughed. "It seemed like every fall when my mother began canning her pickles, she would yell at me, 'Gordon! Have you been in my canning jar rubbers again?'"

Curtis wiped his thick glasses free from the steam that had built up from all his heavy breathing. This was a never-ending problem with glasses. How he hated to wear them, but he had little vision without them. Every year the students in his class would line up at the back of the room. They would take turns reading the eye chart that was taped to the chalkboard. He was so embarrassed.

He couldn't even read the first letter, the big "E."

How he admired Ned who could read the whole chart. To the amazement of all the students, he even read the small print of the publishing company in the lower right-hand corner.

"I sure like the safer feeling of these spring bindings," he said. "I remember when I was about ten, and I lost my ski while up in midair because one of the rubbers broke. What a tumble. It took me forever to find my glasses."

Curtis sidestepped up the front of the jumping platform. The first jump on a new hill was always a special thrill. It was now his to conquer. He enjoyed being first. It was his way of showing others that a new challenge could be accomplished. If he could do it wearing thick glasses, then surely others would follow his example.

The penetrating sun felt good through his black wool sweater and yellow ski cap. Now if only Kenny from school could see that he was no coward. Back and forth he slid his skis, making sure there was no snow sticking to the bottoms. Then he pushed off yelling, "*Ger-on-imo*," as he plunged down the jump.

Bryce and David saw Curtis come over the lower hill airborne with his arms extended in front of his head like a diver. He landed opposite David's shovel, which was set at fifty feet.

"Wow!" exclaimed Bryce. "Did you hear the slap of those skis? I want to try this beautiful hill. What a place to jump."

"Let's get some marking sticks first," suggested David. "We'll measure from the end of the jump out forty feet and then place the sticks in five-foot intervals.

Let's mark up to sixty feet for the longest. We can take turns measuring each other."

The next couple of hours were spent jumping the hill and working their way back up to the top again. One of them would stay at the bottom and mark the length of each jump. Bryce had cut a long poplar sapling to spot each landing. They would mark the jump from the position between both boots on the skis as they touched down.

Each boy extended the length of his first jump. Curtis, as usual, jumped the longest, hitting nearly sixty feet. Gordon was second with fifty. Bryce and David each came in at forty-five feet. Swimmers those two were, but jumpers they were not. All four boys enjoyed competition and the companionship of each other.

The winter weeks drifted by quickly. With basketball, Scouts, and ski jumping, the boys were full to the brim with activities.

One day in mid February, Bryce called Curtis over to the Roosevelt School bulletin board. "Look, Curtis! The junior ski jumping championship is going to be held in Wakefield on March ninth. Why don't you and Gordon enter?"

"Hmmm. That's an eighty-foot hill with a manmade wooden scaffold. I've never jumped on anything but homemade jumps. It sounds scary to me."

Bryce looked at the sign-up list. "Look at this. Your unforgiving Kenny has already entered."

Curtis stared at Kenny's name. "You know, he's been training over there all winter. Doctors' kids sure have all the money. I'd be lucky to even get the entry fee, let alone train over there."

At Sunday dinner, Curtis was eating his favorite roast beef dinner along with riced potatoes and dark brown gravy. How he loved his mom's cooking. Today she had made his favorite dessert, banana crème pie. He talked to his parents about the ski jumping championship. His folks had let him bicycle ninety miles to his grandma's house two years earlier, and last year he had built a raft on Spring Creek with his three best friends. He hoped they would look favorably on this new venture.

"You know, son," his dad smiled, "anyone who can bicycle from Ironwood to Iron River on a one-speed bicycle surely deserves a chance to show his courage in the air. I believe you need opportunities to prove yourself as you become a man. We'll pay your entry fee and take you over to Wakefield for practice."

Curtis had his mother's blue eyes. He looked at her and smiled. "Thank you both so much. I can't wait."

His dad continued, "I have a friend who is a retired ski jumper. Let me give him a call and see if he would be willing to help you. I think it would be great for my son to be a ski jumper.

"A few years ago I discovered a place I call Copper Peak. Right now I'm working on a design for the world's largest ski jump to be built on it. I'm about halfway done. Skiers will be able to jump over four hundred feet. Who knows, maybe my son will get to jump on his father's dream hill."

That evening while Curtis was doing his homework, his dad came up to his room with good news.

"I talked with Joe Maki. He's offered to come with us to Wakefield and coach you the next three Saturdays. Mr. Maki has the hill record of two hundred sixty-five feet over at Iron Mountain."

"Wow!" Curtis' eyes beamed through his wire spectacles as he thought about the fact that Mr. Maki had gone over two hundred feet farther than his own longest jump.

The following Saturday, they stopped to pick up Joe Maki. He invited them into his chalet. It was located in a large forest between Ramsay and Wakefield.

"Curteese, I have soomtheng for yah to youse on da beeg heel. I youse deem when I be yer age fer my furst beeg yump."

Joe Maki was a Finlander. Short, lean, and agile, he had made his mark in Finland ski jumping in the northern part of his country and in Sweden. He had also been a member of the ski troops during the occupation by the Germans.

Curtis took a ski that was leaning against the knotty pine-paneled wall. They were hickory jumpers. There were niches and scratches on the top. He turned them over. There they were, those three deep grooves that identified a jumping ski. The base was clean as a whistle and freshly waxed. He lifted it and felt the heavy weight of hickory. Now when he went down the hill, he knew the skis would track straight and true. He had really been struggling with his lately. They were downhill skis with only one groove. The faster he went, the more his maple skis would chatter and swivel.

"Thank you, Mr. Maki. I'll take good care of them for you. I've never jumped with jumping skis before."

The three Saturdays before the meet came and went.

Mr. Maki had given Curtis many pointers. He kept on repeating one special instruction. "Reemember, style es more eemportant than deestince. Yah want both, but dee judge weel geeve yah much points fer style."

Curtis was constantly hitting jumps in the mid to upper sixty-foot range. This wasn't a whole lot longer than their homemade jump, but the height he got was unreal. Mr. Maki said his style was near perfect.

Saturday, March 9, came, and his whole family, along with Mr. Maki, headed for Wolverine Hill located east of Wakefield. Gordon was also jumping and hitting the upper fifty-foot range. He, too, wore the familiar yellow ski cap that Bryce's mom had knitted for the four boys. Curtis was sharing the special instructions with him.

The hill record was seventy-seven feet. Again Mr. Maki stressed style over distance. When most boys practiced, all they had to go by was the length of their jump. No one said much about style.

In a ski jumping meet, the judges assessed points for a jumper's style and the distance jumped. The maximum was twenty points for each. A perfect score was forty points per jump. Of course, this was from one judge. The judges had to consider the length of the jump and the manner in which you displayed yourself from the top of the scaffold all the way down to the spot where you finished. You were permitted two jumps in which to accumulate these points. The ski jumper with the most points won the competition. With two judges, a perfect score would be eighty points.

The style of the jumper involved stretching out once he was airborne. Both arms were to be extended towards the tips of the skis. This helped in gaining distance as the body penetrated the oncoming air. Upon descending onto the snow-packed slope, the arms were to be extended outward from the shoulders. One ski was to be set slightly forward from the other ski in what was called a three-point telemark landing.

The previous Saturday, Curtis had had another confrontation with Kenny. In fact, Kenny had poisoned the minds of the Wakefield Ski Club about Curtis and his stealing problems. It seemed as though he was never to be forgiven for taking Kenny's BB pistol way back in the fifth grade.

All that morning, they would yell before he jumped, "Here comes the pistol kid," or "Watch out for glass eyes, he may land on you." They even called him the "Ironwood Icabod."

Mr. Maki told him this embarrassment would help him in the meet. He would be used to the pressure and distractions. Kenny's jumps were in the seventies, and people were talking about this kid breaking the hill record.

Joe Maki had even said, "He ees da beeg shot who yumps fer show. He no gat eeny style. You weel see wat dee judge geeve heem fer points. You fly like eeagle. He look like seek cow."

There were thirty-five entries. You were entitled to two jumps. Your total score was based on the length of the jump and style points as determined by the two judges. The prize was the Torval Erickson Trophy and the admiration of the community. In the North Country, ski jumping was as important as football.

On the first jump, everyone was placed in random order. Curtis was number twenty-five, and Gordon number twenty.

"Hi, Curtis," said Gordon wearing a blue reindeer sweater and the familiar yellow ski cap. "I'm nervous as a cat. How about you?"

"I'm ready," he replied. "I hope the wind doesn't play tricks on us. That scaffold is totally unprotected way up there on that rocky bluff."

Both boys assembled in a long line of jumpers near the scaffold above the snow-packed jump. One by one they climbed the steps to the platform. As the skiers descended the jump, Curtis learned there were boys from Canada, Minnesota, Wisconsin, and Illinois. The majority came from Michigan.

It was now Gordon's turn to jump. As he sailed off the end of the ramp, he heard the familiar "*Ger-on-i-mo!*"

That was their courage word. While studying about the American Indians of the West, they had admired the courage of these people whose land was stolen by the American government.

Geronimo seemed an appropriate word expressing freedom of spirit and independence of choice.

The P.A. announced, "...number twenty-five...Curtis Anderson from Ironwood."

Curtis stepped onto the platform, fastened the bindings to his boots, and looked down the J-shaped jump. As usual, he could not see the landing except as it leveled off at the bottom.

Remember, style before distance especially on the first jump. He kept repeating this over and over. He tugged at the bottom of his scarlet wool sweater so no wind would catch any loose material. Gently he fixed his maize ski cap so that it just touched the top of his glasses.

He thought of his older cousin Willard Luba. He had quarterbacked the Iron River Redskins football team with blood flowing continuously from his mouth in a great victory over the Iron Mountain Mountaineers. He remembered how Willard had ironed a white shirt for grandma and hadn't considered it girl's work. And then the sad news they all received. Willard Luba was an Army Air Corps lieutenant trained to fly P-38's. He had just received his "wings," but was killed off the coast of Italy.

Now he was wearing the same red sweater that Willard had worn in high school. He would jump to honor his cousin.

Curtis stood on the flat platform. His five-foot- eleven-inch height and one hundred thirty pounds were considered ideal for ski jumping. Mr. Maki had told him he would get speed from his light weight and distance from his long body. "Now, slide the skis back and forth three times to loosen any sticking snow. Then take three quick steps down the track for speed." These had been Mr. Maki's instructions.

Down the chute he sped. He gained speed with the wind at his back. He looked for the end point of the jump, and then he yelled, "*Ger-on-i-mo!*" as he hurtled outward into endless space. His tall, lean body stretched forward. His hands nearly touched the tips of the skis. As he descended near the bottom of the landing, he slowly brought his arms sideways like the wings of a swan.

"Slap" went the heavy hickory skis simultaneously on what was left of the hard-packed slope. *Oh, how I love the feel of the wind in my face and free falling through the sky.*

Curtis' nearly six-foot frame stood like a statue as he waited for the announcer to declare the distance, style points, and total score. "Distance...seventy-two feet for thirty-six points...style... thirty-eight points...total score from the two judges...seventy-four points."

He could see Gordon throw his arms up in the familiar Churchill victory salute.

He made his way over to his three yellow-capped friends.

"Great jump!"

"Super!"

"Perfect!" all three boys exclaimed.

"You're now in first place!"

"Hey, Curtis! Kenny's number thirty," reported Bryce. "Let's watch him jump before you and Gordon head back up the hill for your final jump."

While they were waiting, Curtis' dad and Mr. Maki came over with words of praise and advice. "Eet was a veery goot yump, Curtees, and yah gat da style like I tell you do." Mr. Maki drew Curtis away from the others and slipped something into his pants pocket. "Thees ees sum jelly wax called paraffin that weel make yer skis fly like lightning. You muss be veery careeful dough, cause eef you don yump at the exact momeent, you weel loose yer balance. When yah go back up da heel, I want yah ta move yer yumping marker back towards yer approach about two feet. Yump wen yah geet to da marker steek. Do yah understand? And reemember, style before deestance."

"Thank you, Mr. Maki. I'll give it my best shot."

"Here comes Kenny!" shouted David.

Down through the air, churning his arms like some wild vulture, came Kenny. He sailed past Curtis' landing spot, and landed beyond the red flag marking the hill record. A shout of excitement and applause came from the huge crowd. Kenny waved his arms in anticipated victory.

The crowd turned silent as they awaited the score. The loudspeaker blared, "Kenny West has broken the hill record with a jump of seventy-nine feet. His score is as follows: forty points for the jump and thirty-four style points. His total score is seventy-four.

"Ladies and gentlemen, after the first round, we have a tie for first place between the two boys from Ironwood, Kenny West and Curtis Anderson."

Curtis smiled. *Same score as mine. How about that.*

Joe Maki was right. Style before distance.

As Curtis and Gordon made their way up the landing, a girl in a long wool purple coat came through the crowd with her mother. Her long wavy brown hair hung down to her shoulders.

"Hi, Curtis! Remember me?"

Her smile and beautiful face, Curtis would never forget.

"Hi, Veronica," replied Curtis. "I remember you from my bicycle trip two years ago. We met at the A&W Root Beer Drive-in at Marinesco.

"Hello, Mrs. Lauti."

"We read about your ninety-mile bicycle trip in the *Ironwood Daily Globe*," said Mrs. Lauti. "It stated you were the first person to bicycle between Ironwood and Iron River. And now you're on a new adventure, ski jumping."

Veronica's deep blue eyes almost matched her coat. Her pink cheeks were beautiful next to the large yellow silk scarf around her neck. "Curtis, you were the most graceful skier of them all. Your three-point landing was perfect."

Curtis blushed. He removed his cap and partly covered his face with it revealing his neatly combed thick golden brown hair.

"I've got to be going. Thanks for coming over."

Veronica smiled again and said, "We'll be watching from near the red flag. That's the hill record marker you know. Let's see you break both records."

At the top of the landing, Curtis quickly waxed his skis with a thin layer of paraffin that Mr. Maki had given him. He also moved his takeoff marker two feet farther away from the end of his previous jump.

All the skiers who had completed round one were now winding their way up the jump like a train of freight cars. This time their jumping order was changed. They were to jump in the order of their total score. This meant that Curtis would be next to last and Kenny would follow him, since they both had the highest point totals.

Curtis didn't like all the waiting even though he was happy about being in the top three. It was now four o'clock, colder, and a crosswind was gusting from north to south. This jump would be different.

I must wait for a lull in the wind when it's my turn. He felt a warm glow inside. The image in his mind was of the girl in the purple coat, Veronica. She was almost like a friend even though this was only the second time they had met. When he looked into her eyes, they seemed endless. It was like being in a cave and looking for the end of it. Somewhere deep down in them, he could sense something he had never experienced before.

Methodically, the skiers were taking turns again. With the colder temperatures and well-worn track, the jumpers were nearly all exceeding their first jumps.

He saw Gordon go by and heard from the loudspeaker that his distance was sixty-five feet. That meant he had increased his jump by eight feet. He was happy for his brown haired crew cut friend. He too battled against physical odds, but instead of thick glasses, he had to contend with being small and lightweight. Curtis admired his friend's courage and quickness.

Curtis calculated in his mind that if he gained eight feet as Gordon had, he would make eighty feet. That would beat Kenny's new record. All the way up the scaffold, Kenny hadn't said a word. There was a big gap between them. What trick was his nemesis planning for him this time?

"Number... twenty-five... Curtis... Anderson of Ironwood," the loudspeaker echoed up the hill. Curtis set his mind to the task. *Stretch the sweater tight, pull the ski cap down to the top of the glasses, glide the skis back and forth three times, three quick steps down the track, and set your sight on the little jumping marker.*

He strained his eyes through the new falling small crystals of snow looking for the marker. It was gone! Kenny must have seen him place it there, and he had taken it to spoil his jump.

Curtis knew this was a faster run. His eyes were watering from the speed and cold air. He sprang from his moving crouched position guessing the marker's location. The liftoff felt perfect. Heat also had been pouring from his body because of his thoughts about Kenny, and maybe a new record jump.

Suddenly both lenses fogged up. He couldn't see anything. Up, up, and down, down, down, he flew with his body arced like the bowsprit of a sleek sailboat. His body was frozen in position like a diving eagle. All he could do was hold his stretched out form and rely on his timing from other jumps for the landing.

As he sailed down the slope, his right eye caught a flash of purple from the sidelines. He remembered that Veronica was wearing a purple coat and said she would be standing near the red flag. And then he heard Joe Maki yell, "Plant yer feeet, Curtees!"

Curtis instantly pulled his outstretched arms to his shoulders and straightened up. There was a loud "slap, slap" as each ski struck the snow in alternating order. Because he was slightly off balance, the right ski landed first. He knew that if he fell, the jump wouldn't count and he would be disqualified. He was riding the landing at a terrific speed and heading for the snow fence towards his right. He was oblivious of the cheering crowd.

Instinctively, he countered the off-balance lean to the right by lifting his left ski and turning the tip trying to catch some wind resistance with his leg. Simultaneously he used his left hand to catch some air also. It worked. Slowly he began pulling away from the fence.

The crowd roared with cheering. They applauded his courage as he glided up to the red snow fence at the end of the landing.

Someone shouted from the other side of the barricade. "Look! He couldn't see! His glasses are all frosted over! He jumped blind."

As word spread through the audience, a strange silence spread over Wolverine Hill. Curtis took his glasses off, removed a handkerchief from his rear pocket, and wiped the frost from them.

The announcer clicked on the P.A. and said, "This is a unique moment, ladies and gentlemen. Curtis Anderson has just set a new hill record for distance. He jumped eighty-five feet. The two judges report forty points for distance and thirty-six points for style. His total score for this jump is seventy-six points. We have one more jumper to end the competition. His previous jump set a new hill record up until now. This should be one grand finale."

Kenny was getting impatient at the top. The wind was blowing strong, and the snow flurries had increased. He heard what Curtis had done and was driven by malice to do better.

Down he came. His blue and red sweater stretched out like a flaming meteor way down the hill. He had really caught an updraft in the wind. Distance he wanted. Another record at any cost. The glory of the longest jump would be his. He flew beyond the mark that Curtis had just set. He went beyond the slope of the hill and set down on the beginning flat part of the landing. With no angle from the slope to carry his weight, the force of the impact shattered his left ski into two long pieces. What was left caught the snow and flipped him into the air. As he landed, the other ski catapulted off. He crashed into the fence to the left of Curtis.

Silence stilled the spectacle as Kenny lay in a heap. Curtis ran over to him.

"You out-jumped the hill, Kenny. Let me help you." Curtis saw blood coming from his face where a splinter from the ski must have struck him. He placed his handkerchief over the wound.

"I'm not sure about my left knee." Kenny's face was white as a sheet. "Please help me up."

Curtis first removed what was left of the broken ski. It was a strange yet calm feeling he experienced as Kenny put his arm around his shoulders. Dr. West met them at the fence as Kenny limped up to it for support.

The crowd of ski lovers applauded when they saw Kenny standing and the sportsmanship of Curtis. There was a constant buzzing among the people as they awaited the results of the day's meet.

All of the ski jumpers were told to assemble at the bottom of the hill in the landing area. The voice from the loudspeaker began. "Today we have witnessed history in the making. Twice the hill record was broken. An almost third time could have seriously crippled Kenny West, but he will heal to jump again.

"Curtis Anderson, from Ironwood, set a new hill record of eighty-five feet jumping blind on his takeoff. It's quite an accomplishment to ski jump with glasses, but when they fog and frost up, that's an amazing feat. Our first-place trophy is awarded to Curtis Anderson with a two jump total of one hundred fifty points."

Shortly after the awards announcement, Curtis was surrounded by his family, Joe Maki, Gordon, Bryce, and David. While they were all talking and celebrating, Kenny came limping up. He walked straight up to Curtis and said, "I've been very unfair and mean to you. I'm sorry I've caused you so much grief since the incident at my birthday party four years ago. I took your jumping marker so I could beat you. Please forgive me."

Curtis extended his hand and shook Kenny's hand. "You're forgiven. That was one unbelievable jump you made. I like your courage. You really went for it."

The scent of lilac was in the air as he turned back towards his friends. There were Veronica and her mother introducing themselves to his family and buddies. Veronica strolled over to Curtis and removed the yellow scarf from around her neck.

"Curtis," she said, "I present you with the yellow scarf of courage for jumping blind on a hill. Please bend forward and receive your award."

He had learned quickly about Veronica's gentle sense of humor from their meeting on his bike trip. She was tall and slender like him, but there were no thick ugly-looking glasses obstructing the beauty of her fine-featured face. He removed his glasses and bowed before her as she tied the soft silk perfumed scarf around his neck.

"There," she said, "the scarf matches the yellow of your ski cap." Her blush was hidden by the color in her cold cheeks. "I must go now, but I'll keep reading the paper for some news about your next adventure."

"Goodbye, Veronica. Ironwood will be playing Wakefield next year in basketball. I play center and hope to see you at the game."

Joe Maki put his arm around the shoulders of Curtis. "Yah learn well and yer style make youse a champeen. I want you to have my old yumping skees. It is a geeft for yah and make me proud. I tink Veronica veery proud of yah too."

Chapter IV

The Shiny Signet Ring

Curtis gazed off through the window of the north-bound train to a forest of mixed hardwoods and evergreens. As he did so, he noticed the reflection of his face and the big thick glasses that made him look different from anyone else in school.

It was a huge handicap in sports. To get around this problem, he played without them, although there were quite a few embarrassing moments. He often thought that he didn't have many friends in school because he looked strange. In grade school, the students used to call him "specks." All that teasing had sent him into the woods at an early age to seek for solitude.

Here in his wilderness, there were no words of rebuke, criticism, or mockery. Trees, the silent sentinels of the woods, fluttering chickadees, and the water of streams gliding under logs and over rocks were his companions.

As he looked at his reflection again, he could see that they did sort of look like magnifying glasses. One thing for sure, he received a lot of attention in school. He was also considered the class clown. Learning to use humor to release his anxiety and focus attention on what he said instead of how he looked enabled him to cope with his appearance.

Oh, well, he thought, *I am loved by my family, Grandma Anderson, and Grandfather Frank.*

This would be the second summer he had left his closest buddies at home. Bryce, Gordon, and David were going to play American Legion baseball again. Curtis had trouble seeing the ball. Again his glasses encumbered him, and the possibility for embarrassment was always present.

As the train chugged along the meandering tracks, he knew that the glory of his life was to be found in the wilderness. He couldn't help wondering, though, *Will this trip to Grandpa Frank's cabin on Kabinakagami (caw bin a caw ga me) Lake be as adventuresome as the bicycle trip to Iron River a few years ago?*

As his oily face leaned against the window, drowsiness crept over his tall one hundred-forty-pound frame. He was nearly six feet tall and skinny as a giraffe. His saving grace was his thick light brown hair neatly parted on the left side and those blue eyes. And he could jump like a gazelle, ski jumping, rebounding in basketball, and catching passes in football. It may not seem like much of an ability, but his teammates admired this jumper who had to play without his glasses in order to compete.

He noticed the Milepost 39 sign. At Milepost 229 he would get off. His two Duluth packs and brand new canoe were all in the baggage car. Closing his eyes, Curtis reviewed the events from his last birthday in January.

His mother, father, brother, and two sisters had blindfolded him after a scrumptious roast beef supper. Then they had led him outside into the garage.

"What's this?" he asked. "I still have Mr. Maki's skis. I smell fresh-cut wood."

Quickly they removed the blindfold. There before him, on two wooden sawhorses, he recognized the long thin strips of white cedar for a canoe. Ever since he had seen his friend Bryce and his dad making a homemade boat, Curtis had wanted to work with his hands and make a cedar-strip canoe.

"Thanks a million, everyone! What's in the box?"

Curtis squinted hard.

"Take a look, son," replied his dad. "It's from Grandpa Frank."

Opening the large cardboard box, Curtis discovered a glossy soft-covered book titled, *Building a Cedar-Strip Canoe*. Underneath the book was a collection of brass brads, hardware, and glue.

The glass of the window was cold on the cheek of Curtis as he mused about the sixteen-foot homemade *Prospector* that lay silent in the baggage car. The shades of tan to brown long inch-wide horizontal strips made for a beautiful work of art. Ash gunwales, moose-hide caned seats, and dark cherry decks were glossed with varnish. Although Curtis had checked it out on a pond, this trip was to be its maiden voyage. He couldn't wait to show it to Grandpa Frank. He had run this stretch of river with his grandpa, but never by himself. Everything would depend on his skills and the level of the water.

As he continued to lean his head against the window, his chin began to droop to his chest. He caught a glimpse of the letter "C" on his signet ring. He loved the Old English style of printing. The swaying motion of the passenger car and the clickety-clack of the tracks lulled Curtis to sleep.

A tapping on his shoulder startled him. "We're almost to Milepost 229. Come on back with me, and I'll give you a hand with your beautiful canoe and the luggage," the conductor announced. "By the way, we've had one dry spring up here. One of my jobs has been to watch for any sparks that might come from the train's smokestack and start a fire. I'm telling you this so you'll be careful with any campfires you make."

As he walked to the rear of the train, the chugging locomotive began to slow. Looking out the window, the movement of the smoke told him that there was a wind from the west. Now he could see the curvature of the river and its sun-laden reflection. What a sight! Soon he would be caught up in its current and alone with the canoe in his beloved wilderness.

Piled alongside the railroad tracks were the glistening canoe, two green Canvas Duluth packs with gear for a month's stay at his grandpa's cabin, two spruce paddles, a fishing pole, and a small tackle box.

Minutes later, with a loud whistle sendoff from the train, Curtis was caught up in the downstream current heading for Lake Kabinakagami. It would be about a day and a half paddle to the cabin. He noticed that the water level was low.

He spoke to the canoe, "Well, here come the scratches and souvenirs from our first solo trip."

The river he was paddling was about twice as wide as the canoe. It was hemmed in on both sides with a mix of black spruce and various pines. Occasionally, there were chasms of rock with class-two rapids. It would empty into the lake within sight of Grandpa Frank's cabin. He couldn't wait to show it off.

Grandpa Frank had taught Curtis to canoe. This was his fifth trip to Canada to see his grandpa, but never before had he gone solo down this river. His dad had told him, "In Lincoln's time, a boy was considered a man when he was sixteen. That's one of the reasons why your mother and I gave you that signet ring. It's your mark into manhood."

The wooden canoe traveled quietly down river. Every now and then they flushed ducks that were still migrating north: cinnamon teal, red heads, mergansers, mallards, and wood ducks. How colorful the heads of these animals appeared.

Curtis recalled his grandpa's last letter reminding him to reverse the ends of the canoe and sit in the bow seat which would now become the rear of the canoe. He had said, "You'll get better steerage because you will be closer to the center of the canoe. Also, don't forget to put your gear towards the bow. If you get in rough water, move the gear more towards the center."

What a teacher his grandfather was to him. Eight different paddle strokes he had learned on previous trips to Ontario. His favorite was the Indian stroke. The paddle never came out of the water. You could control the canoe from one side. It was quiet, yet powerful. Of course, the neat thing about going down river was to let the current do the work. This meant steering by using the paddle as a rudder.

About noon of the second day, Curtis observed a large space ahead with no trees. He knew when he was approaching a lake, even though he couldn't see it. There was that certain expanse of nothing but sky over the treetops. Suddenly he could hear the splashing of waves upon the shore.

Around the bend he came and said, "Wow! Look at those whitecaps."

He looked at his Waltham pocket watch given to him by Grandpa Anderson. Sure enough, it was after ten o'clock.

Invariably, if there was going to be a wind for the day, it seemed to consistently kick in at that time. Even his grandfather had told him, "If you're going to paddle across a large body of water, you better get it done between sunrise and ten o'clock."

At this eastern end of Lake Kabinakagami, the contour of the shoreline was shaped like the horns of a steer. He had just come down the left horn and now entered into its long face. At this spot, the lake was perhaps no wider than a mile across.

Curtis moved the two Duluth Packs from the bow to the middle of his canoe. He was in for a choppy ride, but he could already see his grandfather's cabin. It was nearly midway between both shores. A little less than an hour's paddle should put him at the dock on the lee side of the island and out of the wind.

Abandoning the Indian stroke he poured the coals to his bobbing craft using a combination of the J and Canadian strokes. As he neared the rocky island, he could distinctly see the log cabin, but something was missing. There was no smoke rising out of the beach-stone chimney. Early June still had cold mornings. It was nearly noon. Something didn't seem right; furthermore, he knew his grandfather was expecting him.

Docking the canoe, he hurried up the curved pathway to the cabin. *I hope nothing happened to him like Grandpa Anderson.*

Quickly he opened the door and looked for some sign of life in the main room of the three-room cabin. Nothing. The doors of both bedrooms were open. It was deathly quiet. He entered his grandfather's bedroom expecting the worst. The bed was made neat as a pin with a Hudson Bay red and black striped wool blanket covering it. His heart relaxed a little, and he headed for the guest bedroom. Same thing. Bed neatly made with its Hudson Bay green and black striped wool blanket. Green was his favorite color.

He went outside and headed for the woodpile, checked the woodshed, and ran over to the outhouse. Nothing. And then he remembered. There were supposed to be two canoes overturned on the dock, and he had only seen one.

Hmmm. Maybe he is out fishing, he thought to himself.

Curtis returned to the cabin for one last look-see.

The table was set for two. And then he saw it—a piece of paper propped up against the sugar bowl. It was a note.

> May 30, 1:00
> Dear Curtis,
>
> I broke a front tooth eating a piece of my freshly baked cherry pie. The pain is wicked. I'm heading for Hornepayne and the dentist. It's a three-day

> trip one way. Hope to be back in seven days. Make yourself at home.
>
> Love,
>
> Grandpa Frank
>
> P.S. Don't eat any of that cherry pie unless you want to see the dentist.

The remainder of the day was spent unpacking, splitting firewood, reading from a Curwood novel, and wondering when Grandpa Frank would return. Today was June fifth. That meant that six days had gone by. A three-day trip to town, one day with the dentist, and three days back meant he should return tomorrow.

Early the next day found Curtis in his canoe working the shoreline with his fishing pole. Since the water was still quite cold, he knew that somewhere off from the river mouth the walleye should be clustered in a large school. By slowly trolling a large pikey minnow lure, it wouldn't take long to hook into breakfast.

Sure enough, on his first pass near a rock outcropping, he hooked a keeper. Minutes later he gazed down on a gold-colored walleye about eighteen inches long. This would be breakfast.

By mid-afternoon the temperature had risen to an unbelievable eighty-five degrees. This was indicated by the thermometer anchored to a huge white pine tree located outside the window and opposite the dining table. It was time for a swim. Curtis had a custom of going for an early morning swim before breakfast, but today he had decided to fish instead. A swim the first thing of the day really woke him up.

A short distance out from the dock were several large boulders. Some almost protruded the surface of the lake. The sport was to swim out to them and then take turns diving off each one. The water was still cold from the spring breakup. It was exhilarating, and he felt himself cooling down, but about twenty minutes was all he could take.

Standing on a huge boulder, he took in the picturesque setting. To his left was the island with the red pine cabin built when his grandfather had been a young man. The island was about a mile long and shaped much like an arrowhead. The cabin was located on a small bluff at its eastern end.

To the east were the two rivers, which emptied into a crescent-shaped bay. He had come down the one inlet yesterday.

To the west, the lake stretched its span for five miles before turning northward. There was located the stream his grandfather had taken. They had run its rapids many times, and Curtis had learned his fast-water paddle strokes.

Southward was a dense forest of jack pine and birch interspersed with some tall red and white pine. Gazing back at the bluff on which the cabin was located, he noticed the watermark. The lake was down nearly a foot.

Curtis stood transfixed on the large boulder with his fingers barely dangling in the water. The mixed aroma of smoke from the chimney of the cabin and the pine-scented air filled his whole presence with joy and peace. This was his heaven away from the strange looks of the kids back at school. If they only knew how he could handle a canoe or build a wilderness camp, they would marvel instead of tease him.

He decided to swim to the dock. Suddenly, there was a piercing pain in his left hand. He screamed and plunged into the lake. Slashing with his arms, he swam as fast as he could for the shore. Climbing onto the dock, he looked at his hand. Blood was oozing out in a steady flow all over his fingers. Kneeling down on the weather-beaten dock, he washed it off in the water and looked again. Sure enough, something had cut a partial circle around his gold signet ring. He washed the bright red blood off again. What kind of a creature could have done such a thing, and why around the finger with the shiny gold signet ring?

He walked rapidly up to the cabin trying to stop the blood by applying pressure with the thumb and index finger of his right hand. Inside the cabin, he tore off a strip from a dishtowel and wrapped it around the finger. Locating the first-aid kit, he removed the ring and washed the finger with peroxide. In examining it more carefully, he noticed that the cut was jagged. It must have been made by the sharp teeth of a fish. Why would a fish bite his finger?

He thought about the lures in his tackle box. Artificial lures were made to attract fish, and many of them were silver or gold in color. That had to have been the reason for the fish attack. It had been attracted to his finger because of the shiny gold signet ring. With the finger hanging below the ring, the fish would have considered it food of some kind.

Wait until my mom and dad hear about this. The ring of manhood teaches its first lesson, pain.

He knew Bryce, Gordon, and David would believe him, but this would be considered a colossal fish story by the other students at Roosevelt School.

After bandaging the wound, Curtis spent the rest of the day taking it easy. Fortunately, it was on his left hand, which meant it wouldn't interfere with fishing.

That evening found him trolling the shoreline around the island keeping a watchful eye out for his grandpa. The fishing was a bonanza. He caught about a dozen walleye. He kept two of them for the next day. "Only keep what you can eat," his grandfather had continuously advised.

Even though he was on the lee side of the island, he observed that the wind had really kicked up from the south. He headed for his grandpa's cabin. Sleep would come easy tonight, and surely Grandpa would return tomorrow. With the brisk wind flapping the light blue curtains through the windows, Curtis crawled into bed.

Sometime during the moonless night, Curtis awoke coughing. *I smell smoke!* He thought. Reaching for the flashlight, he put on his heavy wire-rimmed glasses. Walking into the main room of the cabin, he noticed a bright glow coming through the south window.

"It's got to be a forest fire." He coughed again. "I wish Grandpa was here. He would know what to do."

He looked at his pocket watch; it was nearly two o'clock.

Again he could hear his grandpa's words from past experiences. "When you don't know what to do, think for yourself. Remember, in the wilderness, it's your skills and thinking against all the forces of nature. If you master the skills and give thought to each predicament, you will survive. And if this should fail in some way, pray.

"Remember, you are more than a tree or a bear; you are spirit. God is a Spirit. Prayer is a way your spirit can talk to God. If you listen or depend on Him, He will provide a solution to your need. The Puritans called this Providence.

"And another thing," he continued, "there is no such thing as mother nature. A wilderness person knows this concept is a myth. Nature is not human. It is neither cruel nor gentle, male nor female, except as it exists in the minds of people. You learn all you can about the natural laws of this earth. Then you develop your skills to cope with them.

"Remember the great asset we have over nature, the ability to think. If we use our minds, we can solve most of the problems we encounter."

Curtis lit the kerosene lamp, which was sitting on the red oilcloth-covered table. His mind told him that the south wind would push the flames towards the island. Even though the cabin was a half-mile from that shoreline and all those pine trees, sparks could fly though the air and burn the cabin to the ground. This was no place to stay.

Quickly he dressed. Grabbing an empty Duluth bag, he quickly filled it with his tent, sleeping bag, matches, axe, saw, some food supplies, and anything else that came to mind. He removed Grandpa Frank's rifle from the wall and took all the ammunition from off the shelf. He also took his grandpa's Bible from the table. These were two things that he knew his grandpa treasured. Closing all of the windows, he blew out the lamp and headed down to the dock with the gear.

Now his hope was to paddle the length of the lake before the fire invaded the shore. Once into the outlet, he felt the speed of the current would take him safely out of the fury of the fire. It would be a race of five miles that had to be won.

It was a roly-poly ride across the short half-mile stretch to the southern shoreline. Once that had been attained, he stayed out just far enough to keep from hitting deadfalls and rock outcroppings along the edge of the lake. He paddled rapidly towards the western outlet.

About an hour later he heard that familiar voice of the rapids. Even in the darkness, there was no mistaking the sound he had heard many times before. Rivers are like highways. You listen and you recognize certain sounds as belonging to their users. Now he entered the noise of the river. He became alarmed at the redness of the clouds up ahead. It would normally have been a difficult paddle down this stream, but the illuminated sky enabled him to maneuver with a minimum of scrapes on boulders.

About a half hour into his downward descent towards Hornpayne, Curtis swung around a long bend and received a blast of hot wind and smoke that nearly took his breath away. And then he saw the inferno. Midway down this stretch of water, the river narrowed. There was no river up ahead. It had disappeared. Tall jack pines were burning with flames streaking like northern lights. Flaming trees had fallen across the river barricading any possibility of getting through. Sparks were flashing in the air like a spewing volcano. The water was hissing from the falling trees and embers. The fire was a consuming dragon. Nothing could escape its wrath.

Captivated by this force of nature, Curtis quickly moved to the center of the canoe, fell to his knees, and back paddled with rapid strokes. Using a draw stroke, he turned the canoe and headed back upstream fighting the current as he went. Fortunately, the canoe did not have much gear. It floated high in the water.

He looked at his watch. It was now four o'clock.

That meant he had been on the river for thirty minutes, but going back to the lake would take at least twice as long.

The forest fire was creeping closer to this part of the river. Dip-pull, dip-pull, dip-pull—with all the strength of his upper body, he slowly gained the stretch to the first of three rapids. Here the water was moving so rapidly that he couldn't go forward. Jumping out of the canoe, he began to push it forward. Fortunately, the rapids were shallow. Once he conquered this stretch, he would jump back into the canoe and paddle to the next set of rapids.

The wind was hot on his port side, and embers were falling like snowflakes in a blizzard. He was beginning to feel stings on his face. This was a hornet's nest of flying debris. He began to cough continuously. Jumping in and out of the canoe did have one benefit. It kept him wet and cool except for his face. He decided to drench his hat. The water running down his face was a gratifying relief.

He plowed through the last rapids that served as the entrance to the river. The pine trees on his right were aflame. At last he made the lake. Now he would be safe from the force of the fire. The bandaged finger on his left hand was sopping wet and stained red. He needed to put a fresh bandage on it soon.

Panting for air, Curtis laid his paddle on the gunwales. He was exhausted. His clothing was a mix of water from pushing the canoe through the rapids and sweat. Gray and white ashes polka-dotted his clothing leaving tiny pinholes. Looking eastward in the direction he had come through the night, he could see the first hint of sunrise. The wind had disappeared, but the crackling of the forest fire sounded like burning split-cedar kindling. Smoke shrouded the lake. The north shore of the river was still green. The unknown expanse of this part of the lake was his only choice of escape.

Grabbing the wet paddle, he noticed something swimming in the water from the fireside of the bay. Whatever it was, it could barely move. He J stroked the canoe into its path and waited. And there it was, a baby red fox maybe a foot long.

Using his paddle, he lifted the waterlogged creature into the canoe and set it down in the bow. How about that? He had rescued his favorite animal of the woods. They headed north up the long arm of the lake into unknown territory.

By late afternoon, the sun had dried out both passengers in the cedar-strip canoe. The petite fox had begun to crawl around and now was perched on the Duluth pack.

"Aye, little fox! I'm thinking you need a name, and I want a friend to keep me company. How about I call you Blaze? That name not only matches your fur, but the fire storm you escaped." Hopefully, his new companion would stay with him until he found his grandfather.

As the sun settled westward, the end of the lake came into view, and ahead lay an island with a sandy shore. He spied a quantity of driftwood that would supply them fuel for frying one of the two walleye he had brought along.

They had paddled all day leaving the fire at water's edge. Only the smoke had continued to creep along with them into this unknown expanse to the north.

The first priority Curtis attended to was replacing the dressing on his finger. It had swollen considerably, and the lacerations from the fish had turned red. The dry bandage felt good, but the throbbing was giving him a headache.

Blaze was acting more like a curious raccoon than a fox. The little rascal really enjoyed the baked fish he had fried up for supper.

The next day found Curtis and Blaze canoeing into a sluggish outlet. The lay of the land was changing from that of bluffs and rocky shoreline to flat grassy areas and black spruce trees. The sky was powder blue with puffy white clouds slowly moving in from the southwest. The tinge of smoke still penetrated the cool morning air.

Blaze was curled up on the warm canvas Duluth pack peering at the unknown interior.

All morning long Curtis paddled the slow, meandering waterway. His compass was mounted on top of a crossbeam. He had learned this trick from his grandpa. It gave quick access to the direction headed while still paddling.

"It sure beats taking it out of your pocket all the time," he told him.

It indicated they were heading north. That was just what Curtis had hoped. He had no map, but remembered that the town of Hornpayne was situated northwest of Kabinakagami Lake. His hope was to find an intersecting river that would eventually flow westward. From there he would inquire from some fisherman or cabin and get instructions.

"Aye, Blaze! Do you like this adventure you're on with a white man? My name is Curtis Anderson. We're going to find Grandpa Frank who went to see a dentist three days' journey from our cabin. Do you like my homemade cedar-strip canoe? I built this myself, but don't you go to teething on the gunwales. I know how you critters like to chew on wood."

Blaze would perk up his ears and look at Curtis whenever he said the word "Blaze."

Although the flow of the water was sluggish, Curtis knew that it was an outlet from the lake by the bent direction of the grass, which was clearly visible underneath the canoe. Little by little the terrain began to revert back to rocks and hills. The stream narrowed and increased in speed. Occasional tributaries started feeding the river.

At noon they stopped for a bite to eat near the entrance to a canyon. He examined the sore finger. It had swollen more. The only way to relieve the pain was to put it in the cold water.

As they entered the narrow canyon, Curtis knew this could spell trouble unless he first scouted the area ahead. He couldn't see it, but his ears picked up the sound of rapids. Even Blaze heard the churning of water on rock and cocked his head sideways.

Taking the bow rope, Curtis made a leash for Blaze. "There now, little fella. I'll be back after I've checked out the rapids up ahead."

Climbing up the steep reddish brown bluff, Curtis walked the edge of the canyon. "Impossible!" he said. "Too much white water. The risk is not worth it. I'll have to find another way."

Retracing his steps, he noticed a large creek coming into the river from the west. That was the direction he wanted to go, but it would mean the hassle of going upstream into the current. It was wide enough, he thought.

Continuing to walk the massive bluff to the west, he could see for miles. The creek was hidden for the most part, yet there were openings where it looked navigable. And then he saw its source, a large lake studded with islands. It would be worth a try.

Back at the canoe, he untied Blaze. "We're going to 'Go west, young man.' The creek looks doable."

With Blaze in the canoe, Curtis paddled up river to the outlet of the creek. From there he jumped out of the canoe and began towing with a rope up the shallow gravel- strewn stream.

"You just hold on, fella. If all goes well, we're going to be camping on an island tonight."

The water was frigid, and it didn't take long for his feet to go numb. At first the stream was free of logjams. Around a few bends where the water slowed, there wasn't enough force to drive the deadfalls out of the way. This required using the small bow saw and axe that fortunately had been packed out of habit the night of the fire. It usually took two cuts to make an opening. Once in a while one cut would dislodge the end of a tree creating an opening.

The stream meandered near the base of the bluff. The shade was the ideal habitat for mosquitoes.

"I forgot the mosquito dope," yelled Curtis back to Blaze.

Occasionally he would yelp, and this was one of those times. The mosquitoes descended like a flock of geese on a cornfield. It got so bad that he just had to stop. *Think—— think,* he said to himself. *How do we get rid of mosquitoes when there doesn't seem to be a way?* And then he remembered the Indian method. Rub mud on your face and any other exposed skin. This he did, but now the swarming insects sought the blood-stained bandaged finger.

Hour by hour went by, and the struggle went on. It was torture now. His finger swelled larger. Bark and sawdust littered the interior of the canoe. His hands were scraped from hoisting the canoe over half sunken logs. One thing the teasing in school from his younger years had taught him was perseverance. Keep moving on and don't stop until you've achieved your goal.

"Per-se-vere!" his grandfather would say.

Sometimes there were pools made from logjams. Once that barricade was portaged around, it was a luxury to get into the canoe and paddle for awhile. This was done repeatedly. Then began the cycle of pulling with the rope all over again. More sawing, more chopping of dead branches pointing as lances from logs. It never seemed to end. With the obstacles, however, he noticed that he was becoming quite accomplished with the routine. Portaging the tangle wood was impossible.

As they continued to move upstream, he could spot the obstacle from a distance. By the time they got to the spot, he knew exactly what to do to solve the problem.

As the hours on his pocket watch rotated towards evening, long shadows began extending from the trees. The wind picked up.

"Aye, my friend Blaze. Does the wind and the sun not tell us that maybe we are nearing the lake I saw from that red granite bluff?"

Removing his mud and sawdust smeared glasses, Curtis faced his strongest ear upstream. "Do I hear the smashing of waves on the shore?" Looking up into the rapidly moving clouds, he saw an eagle. "Ah, huh! Where there are eagles, you'll find fish. We must be getting close."

He dug into his pack for the canteen. After downing the remaining half of it, he ate a yellow delicious apple. He gave little Blaze a piece of venison jerky to chew on.

"Forward and onward, upward and downward," he yelled. "Let's have beans, hardtack, and some of Grandpa's pit-less cherry pie for supper. Watch your teeth now!"

As the horizon began to turn orange, the wind from the lake drove the mosquitoes further inland. Frothing whitecaps came into sight. White birch trees framed windows to the lake that stopped Curtis in his tracks. An island could be seen through two of them. What a painting this would make. It was to be their home for tonight, and he couldn't wait to rest his bruised body. A fire to dry the grimy clothes would be his other friend at this day's end.

Curtis lay in his warm sleeping bag listening to the wind driving the whitecaps to the eastern shore of this unknown lake. Where was Grandpa tonight? *I wonder if my folks have heard about the forest fire in Ontario?* He tried to keep his hand elevated on the Duluth Pack. The throbbing wasn't quite as bad that way.

In the early morning dawn, there was a scratching sound outside the entrance to the Whelen tent. Quickly he realized it had to be Blaze. He pulled up the netting to let him in. Looking through the nylon netting, he could see the sky was gray. A glance at the lake told him that on this day they would be wind bound. The waves looked frightening, and he knew he had no skill equal to that obstacle.

"It looks like a storm, Blaze. I'm going to put up the tarp over the fire just in case. Besides, I'm bushed. A day in camp will do us both good. My finger sure needs some healing time."

Blaze walked over and started licking his hand. Their trials together were making them friends. The licking prompted him to remove the bandage and let Blaze lick the infected finger. Somewhere he had read that animals lick their wounds to bring about healing. It was worth a try.

The reprieve in camp was energizing to the two bodies that had suffered from the stress of the fire and yesterday's upstream battle. Having a generous supply of wood available and sitting under a tarp was an adventure in itself. The small site was protected by a massive granite bluff equal to nearly the height of the birch trees near the tent. The gale-driven waves poured out their oxygen. There were times when breathing seemed to penetrate deep into the lungs. And then there was the fragrance of the wood burning from the campfire. Here on this spot, the two of them had a ringside seat to the slashing of the storm and the warmth from a friendly fire.

In spite of the throbbing finger, this was the world of the wilderness that Curtis dearly loved. He remembered the words of James Oliver Curwood, his favorite author, "No man can have a truly meaningful life until he comes in contact with nature."

Two days later, the storm vanished sometime during the night. With water vapor steaming from the lake, Curtis used the mounted compass to navigate westward. The lake was perhaps ten miles long and located on an east-west corridor.

A new problem had developed. When he had left the cabin, Curtis had hastily figured provisions for five days. The normal three-day trip would have a cushion of two extra days. He hadn't planned on the fire barricade and this detour. He calculated that he had been out for four days. There was food left for only one more day unless he rationed it. True, he had his grandpa's rifle, but they had seen no game.

Taking stock of the food left in the Duluth Pack, he came up with the following items: one ring of hardtack, half a chunk of cheese, two apples, some raisins, and a little venison jerky. Of course, there was no shortage of water. He would ration everything and eat only when absolutely necessary. He chided himself over and over again for not remembering to bring the fishing tackle.

At least they were headed in the right direction, but where they were he had no idea. The morning passed. As they approached the western shore, Curtis started looking for a stream wide enough to exit the lake. The sun had evaporated all of the steam. There were small islands and isolated weed banks arrayed all over the place. The countryside had definitely changed to flat land. It reminded him of their exodus from Lake Kabinakagami. The question was would there be a way out from this lake?

They worked the shoreline meandering among the small inlets and deadfalls. Spring had sprung its annual orchestra. There was entertainment galore from ducks, geese, swans, frogs, loons, crows, hawks, peepers, and a moose with her calf.

The brown-striped canoe approached a small bay.

Curtis looked down into the water for any sign of bent grass indicating a flow of water. Up ahead was a hummock of grass and in it a circle of white and gray downy feathers. Coming closer, there appeared eggs in some sort of nest. Blaze stood up on the front seat with his paws on the deck whimpering. Suddenly there was a loud squawking sound coming from behind them. A bird was headed right for the canoe flying low over the water.

Curtis ducked as a Canadian goose zipped by his head.

Blaze started yipping. Another goose came from a different direction mimicking the same action. Curtis took his paddle ready for battle if the bird came back. Like crop dusting airplanes, both geese came towards the canoe again. Curtis tried to paddle and swat at the black and gray creatures at the same time.

There was a sudden thud as the canoe hit the muddy bank of the nest. Swoosh came the first goose and partly hit the blade of the upturned paddle. He crouched low in the canoe as the second goose cruised across the water approaching the canoe from the bow. Suddenly a white stream of liquid spurted out from the belly of the goose. One whiff of the stuff told Curtis that this gander had released the contents from his bladder. The spattering of white went the whole length of the canoe making it appear like some kind of monster skunk.

Curtis turned his head in the direction of the nest. A circle of feathers was filled with about a half dozen off-white eggs. So this is what the warfare was all about.

Swoosh, the geese went squawking by the canoe again. Quickly he pushed off from the little island. Several times the geese attacked. The little fox and Curtis crawled into the bottom of the canoe and remained stationary. Only his hand with the swollen finger remained in the cold water.

"We'll just lay low for awhile," Curtis spoke to Blaze. "Maybe if we don't move, they will leave us alone."

As the sun began to move past its noon zenith, Curtis took a peek at the nesting area. The goose was now sitting on her eggs. The gander continued to harass the canoe by swimming around it. Every time he would get up to paddle, the gander would attack again. They continued to drift.

It was a hot afternoon. Taking out his watch, he noted it was three o'clock. They had been prisoners for nearly three hours.

Looking down in the water, Curtis saw the sign he had been searching, bent grass. It was pointed towards the woods up ahead. This meant that the canoe had caught the flow of a slow-moving outlet. His hope had become a reality.

Slowly the slight current pulled the homemade canoe away from the mother incubating the newly laid eggs. By late afternoon, the gander had returned to its mate, and the canoe's twosome were into the more rapid flow of a wide river. Curtis continued to move with the flow. It was a continuous series of waterways; however, there was no place to camp. The whole area was one gigantic swampland.

"Aye, my friend Blaze. Have you ever camped in a canoe before? We have until eleven o'clock before it's too dark to see. Let's hope we'll find some place to pitch our tent." Curtis began to whistle softly.

Two long days passed with scant rations. On this day there had been nothing to eat. In his haste to leave the cabin, Curtis had forgotten the fishing gear. He hadn't anticipated the fire jam in the river. True, he had Grandpa Frank's rifle, but he wasn't about to shoot either the moose or calf they had seen. Maybe they could shoot a fish.

Curtis sat in the canoe like an Egyptian Sphinx. His left arm hung limp in the water. He was burning with fever from the infection. He kept repeating, "Got to get some food...must drink more water...can't make it any further."

He had beached the canoe on a sandy spit of land, which extended out from a small, shallow bay. Too tired to move, he slept.

As soon as the canoe landed, Blaze had jumped out and headed into the bush. He had gotten wind of something.

A short time later, he reappeared in front of the grounded canoe. Curtis was still asleep. Blaze began to whimper. Curtis slowly opened his eyes. He stared at the little fox. In its mouth was a freshly killed rabbit, and it was a plump one.

Curtis smiled. "Good boy, Blaze. We're going to have supper tonight."

After cleaning and skinning the rabbit, Curtis cut a stout branch from a birch tree. He scraped it clean of the bark and pointed each end. This skewer he ran through the rabbit. There was ample firewood scattered along the shore for roasting.

He rummaged through the Duluth Pack for matches, and then he remembered there were none left. He heard Grandpa

Frank's voice again. "Think, think, think, and try to remember the knowledge you have stored in that mental library of yours."

Curtis thought back to his readings from the *Boy Scout Handbook*. There had been a chapter on outdoor survival. Several ways were mentioned about starting fires without matches. He took a quick glance at the sun. The only thing that he had that might work was his pocket watch. He had received it after the death of Grandpa Anderson. It was a large silver Waltham with Roman numerals. It now read 6:00 o'clock p.m.

He screwed off the glass facing of the old watch. Next, he gathered some birch bark and tore it into long curly slivers. After placing these in a small pile, he collected some dry twigs and arranged them into a teepee around the birch bark.

Kneeling down beside this arrangement, he placed his left hand with the blood-stained bandage near the fire starter for balance. It was throbbing painfully. Carefully, he brought the lens from the watch down to a piece of birch bark. By angling the upper side of the glass towards the sun, a tiny pinpoint of light appeared on the thin paper birch bark.

Blaze kept sniffing the freshly cleaned rabbit, not understanding why they couldn't eat it raw. He ate all his food raw.

The beam of sun was magnified to a dot so small, it didn't seem possible this could produce a fire. Suddenly a curl of smoke moved upward. Then a hole appeared in the bark, and around this hole glowed a red circle. Before you could say, "jack rabbit," the tinder burst into flame.

With the rabbit roasting on its skewer, Curtis headed towards some nearby cattails. Taking his Marbles sheath knife, he began digging up roots. Attached to each was a bulb much like that of a tulip.

"Aye, Blaze! Did you know that these bulbs taste like potatoes? We're going to make it, my friend. One way or another, we're going to find Grandpa Frank." Curtis started whistling softly a favorite song, *Home on the Range*.

The next morning was the ninth day since he had left the cabin. He woke up with his t-shirt soaked with perspiration. He tried to get up, but nearly fainted. The finger throbbed. He looked at it. A fluid filled sac had formed around the fish cut. The color was changing from dark red to purple. This meant the probability of gangrene.

He looked at Blaze. "I have no knowledge of how to fix my problem. I must get to a doctor, or I'm afraid I will lose my finger." He sorted through the Duluth pack and found the whetstone. Taking the knife from its sheath, he sharpened the blade until it was sharp as a razor. Next, he took the knife and lanced the bulging finger. The puss flowed out quickly. He let Blaze lick the finger again. He lay down and rested for a spell.

By late that morning, they had traveled through a continuous shallow waterway. It was part stream and part marsh. It progressed westward. Rock outcroppings began to appear along the banks. The stream narrowed. As it did, the current increased.

The sun poured out its heat like a blast furnace upon his olive flannel hat. Blaze repeatedly lapped up water by leaning over the gunwale. Curtis followed the fox's lead by cupping his hand and doing likewise.

The new glossy cedar-strip canoe was now a collection of black scars, chipped-out gouges, and spider-webbed scratches. Jostling over logs, through brush, and scraping over shallow water had altered its newness into that of a relic. It looked like an antique, yet the *Prospector* handled like the seasoned canoe of a Chippewa.

Trailing his left arm from the wrist down into the cold water again brought relief. Curtis lifted his eyes to the west, but all was a blur. All of the water before him looked like tinfoil. Some mysterious force was overcoming him.

He thought of Grandfather Frank and began whisper whistling his grandpa's favorite hymn *How Great Thou Art*. And then he saw his grandpa's face. He could almost touch his gray whiskers.

"One last piece of advice, son. Remember this, when all else fails, prayer prevails."

Curtis prayed out loud. "Dear God. I have tried my best. I am so tired. My finger hurts, and I'm hungry. I am beginning to fail. I can't see clearly. Please deliver me from all my troubles. I ask this in the name of your son, the Lord Jesus Christ. Amen.

"I have to rest, Blaze. You keep watch. If you see any sign of human life, you tell me in your own language. I'll understand."

Curtis sat down in the bottom of the canoe with his back resting against the stern seat. He bent his head down to avoid the intense glare of the sun from off the water. The shiny gold signet ring, hanging on a shoelace around his neck, reflected a brilliant ray of yellow light. It brought back hope and images of his family and his three best friends; Bryce, Gordon, and David. He even saw Veronica again with her pink cheeks and deep blue eyes presenting him with her yellow scarf.

Curtis slept. Blaze climbed down from his favorite spot on top of the Duluth Pack and crawled under the bow seat. Hours passed as the sun moved into the west along with the canoe. It drifted with a slight current mile after mile. A slight breeze crept up from the south. The waterway turned in a long arc away from the sun. Turtles slept on dry logs. Unknown to Curtis, his trailing left arm acted as a rudder keeping the canoe away from the windward bank of the long channel.

The bobbing *Prospector* exited the river channel and entered a huge lake. The increasing wind began pushing the sleeping twosome northward out into the choppy expanse. There was no shoreline ahead, only endless water. The canoe turned broadside and began rocking like a cradle.

The noisy waves woke Blaze. He crawled up onto the seat and began to whine. In looking about with his keen eyes, he spied a bright flashing reflection. It was many miles away and near the western shore.

The waves continued slapping the canoe broadside. Whitecaps were visible a short way ahead. Blaze whimpered again. He crawled back and began tugging on the red flannel shirt of his captain.

Curtis woke with a startled cry upon seeing the rough water ahead. Grabbing the blonde spruce paddle, he turned the canoe abruptly into the wind and headed for the protection of the trees along the shoreline. Water broke over the bow. Blaze was drenched with one wave. He looked like a soaked cat. Curtis laughed. The cold water spraying over the canoe felt good.

"I can see again, Blaze!" he yelled. "At least the haziness is gone."

Finally they gained the protection of the tree-lined shore. He beached the canoe and emptied it of the water from this huge new unknown lake. Curtis grabbed a towel from the pack and dried the skinny critter off.

"Aye, thanks for waking me, my friend. Hey, I smell something sweet. I may be as blind as a bat without my glasses, but God gave me a nose that can smell like a bird dog's. I bet we have lilacs around here."

A short walk into the woods revealed an open grassy area. There before them stood a large drooping lavender lilac bush and from it a picturesque petite bay.

"Makes me think of Grandma Anderson, little fella. She always smelled like a lilac bush when she and Grandpa Anderson went to town on Saturdays. What's this? I can smell something else. Bet your bottom dollar there are raspberries nearby."

A search along the edge of the clearing revealed scores of raspberry plants hanging fully loaded with various shades of the red fruit. What a delicious feast. Curtis began to wonder if this gigantic lake would have people living in cottages. Even this site very well could have had a cabin on it at one time.

As they continued to paddle the rocky coast, Curtis noticed that Blaze was acting strangely. He was standing up with his legs on the bow seat and deck looking off in the distance. It was as though he was on point like a hunting dog.

"What's wrong, Blaze? What do you smell?"

Curtis looked off into the horizon. He saw a shimmering flash. It was like a mirror reflecting back light.

"I see it! I see what you see, Blaze! It must have something to do with people. Maybe it's the window of a cabin."

Curtis had little strength left. A current of energy surged through his body at the expectation of the strange flashing. Holding the paddle halfway down the shaft, he paddled using his right hand. The left hand continued to drag in the cold water helping to relieve the pain. Occasionally, he would hold the infected finger near the shoulder to decrease the swelling and warm it up. There were no more bandages. The finger had turned deep red and swollen to nearly twice its normal size.

The lake was immense. Islands were scattered like a broken bag of jellybeans on a floor. The sun had moved towards its early evening haze. The smell of pine lofted by the wind gave its familiar comforting scent to the wilderness. That particular fragrance was strong on hot summer days. The intensity of the sun's rays upon the dark crevices of its trunk would ooze the pitch to the surface leaving blisters of resin. Even the needles left their residue of sticky substance upon the forest floor.

For some time now, the reflective object had been obscured by a long narrow peninsula. As the homemade canoe approached the cape, Curtis stopped paddling. Blaze stood erect at the bow. On the far shoreline was the bright reflection. Now there was something more. There were two colors barely visible: blue and yellow.

Curtis grabbed the paddle with renewed hope and began paddling with both hands. The canoe gushed forward with each stroke. Ahead, the blue color was shaped crossways. In the middle was the shiny reflection.

Suddenly Curtis yelled out at Blaze. "It's a plane! It's a floatplane. We're saved, Blaze; we're saved!"

And then he cried. His shoulders shook as the tears poured forth from his bronzed face. They landed on his brown muscled arms. Removing his thick gold-rimmed glasses, Blaze could see that his friend's eyes were nearly the same color as the light blue sky.

"Oh, how I thank God, Blaze. It's just like Grandpa said, 'When all else fails, prayer prevails.'"

Within the hour, Blaze and Curtis approached the dock where a blue and yellow Dehaviland float plane was moored. A tall elderly man wearing khaki pants and a green short-sleeved shirt was waiting. He was hatless, and on his face he wore thick silver-rimmed glasses.

"Hello the canoe! I saw you coming across those choppy waves from Piney Point. You have a fine Canadian paddle stroke. At first I thought you had a young dog for a companion, but now I can see it's a beautiful red fox."

"His name is Blaze. I found him swimming during the forest fire. I'm hurt. Could you help me with my infected finger? My name is Curtis Anderson, and I've been lost for nine days."

"I sure can. My name is Dr. Peterson. It must be Providence that brought you to me. Let's get you up to the cabin."

Three days later the swelling had declined. Dr. Peterson had lanced the finger and tended to the injury with meticulous care. Curtis had slept like a hibernating bear waking only at the prodding of the doctor for food. Dr. Peterson said he ate like one, too. Blaze had recovered more quickly and had found a playmate with the doctor's golden retriever.

Parts to repair the airplane had been flown in during this time.

"You know, Curtis, I wouldn't have been here if my plane hadn't malfunctioned. It's quite amazing, isn't it? The next cabin is thirty miles from here. Now that my plane is repaired, what do you say I fly you back to Lake Kabinakagami. If the cabin is burned down, I'll take you over to Hornepayne. You can inquire there about your grandpa or catch the train to return home."

With the battered but not broken cedar-strip canoe lashed to one of the plane's floats, they headed for Grandpa Frank's cabin.

"I've flown over your lake a few times before. We should be there in about forty-five minutes. We'll soon know if the forest fire destroyed the cabin. I'm going to follow the river up from Hornepayne just in case your grandpa is on it looking for you."

As they followed the river, all was a patchwork quilt of green forests and deep blue lakes. They crossed over a massive rocky bluff; the west side of the river turned into a charred wasteland. The forest fire had turned the countryside desolate like the back side of the moon.

"There's the lake up on the right," pointed Curtis. "Look at the south side. It's as black as coal."

"And look how that other bluff to the east prevented the fire from going any further," shouted Dr. Peterson. "We'll soon know if the cabin is still standing."

Curtis admired the doctor. They both had similar physical traits. He too was thin, had thick lenses in his glasses, and loved the wilderness. If Dr. Peterson could become a medical doctor with thick glasses, maybe Curtis could achieve his dream also. His desire was to become a forest ranger.

The blue and yellow Dehavilland approached the island from the west side of the lake. It was an encouraging sight. The island was entirely green. The plane zoomed over the cabin. Making an abrupt banking turn towards the charred south shore, they half circled and landed on the lake.

Out from the cabin came a nearly bald-headed man with a gray beard. He was a stocky fellow wearing green pants hung by red suspenders.

"That's him! That's Grandpa Frank! Oh, I thank God my prayers have been answered, and thank you, Dr. Peterson."

The airplane taxied up to the dock. Grandpa grabbed the wing to steady the plane. Out crawled Curtis with his left arm in a sling. In his other arm he carried Blaze. Around the furry neck of the red fox, dangling from a shoestring, was the shiny signet ring.

Grandpa Frank broke into a broad smile with one front tooth missing. "Well, I'll be buffaloed! Welcome home, Curt."

Chapter V

Cave-in

The four boys were sitting on the deep green steps leading up to the porch of Bryce's home. David wore his familiar tight fitting T-shirt, revealing even more muscles than he had last year in his tapered upper body. He often thought muscles were a better choice over being handsome like his friend, Gordon. David sported a crew cut similar to Gordon's, but his partner's brilliant green eyes were like viewing a male humming bird among the white blossoms of an apple tree. Bryce and Gordon had similar blond hair, but Bryce always seemed to look like the head of a beaver thrust fresh out of the water.

Curtis stood up, pushed two fingers of his right hand against the bottom of his thick-lensed glasses, and walked down the steps. Stepping on the sidewalk and turning towards his friends, they all looked up. This was his style. It seemed to his buddies that whenever Curtis had something important to say, he stood. Maybe it was his dad's strict teaching about etiquette. Even in the classroom he stood when answering a question.

In spite of the cumbersome heavy glasses and lanky frame, it was his neatly combed hair that was more obvious. Streaked with wisps of blond, it was becoming brown like the tannic acid waters of the Montreal River. He continued to be embarrassed about his glasses and oily skin. He parted his hair on the left side and sculptured a most perfect wave at the front with his comb. It was his trademark.

"Guess what, fellows? Last Saturday I discovered a gold mine. You know that cave-in that's fenced behind my Uncle Anderson's Farm. Well, I did it."

"No, you didn't," challenged Bryce. "You know your folks would be alarmed if you went down into that old iron mine cave-in."

"I know, I know," replied Curtis, "but there was a good reason. You remember that our science teacher, Mr. Mertz, gave us a research assignment of collecting rock specimens for our unit on geology. Would you believe it, I have half of my collection already. Look at this." Curtis took from his tan jacket pocket a rock. It was the size of an apple, and it gleamed golden in the sun.

"Let me see it." Gordon walked down the steps and examined the specimen. "It's heavy and sure looks like gold."

"I know what that is!" exclaimed Bryce. "It's 'fool's gold.' We have a piece on our bookcase in the house."

"You're right, Bryce. I showed it to Uncle Willie and he told me the same thing. It has fooled many people because of its golden luster."

Gordon brushed back his crew-cut. "I suppose you're going to tell us that you collected this rock and all of the others from that old sinkhole."

"Yup. Let me tell you what happened. I crawled under that rusty old barbed wire fence and worked my way down into that big cave-in. It was amazing how easy it was. As I stepped from boulder to boulder, I began noticing smaller rocks all over the place. It's interesting how a teacher sets your mind to thinking about things you never thought about before."

"And that's when you collected your specimens?" queried David. "I suppose now with your big head start you'll also go for the extra credit."

"Let me tell you, David. We all could get our rock samples over there. I filled my pockets full. Each one is different in some way. There's hematite, magnetite, nickel, quartz, shale and some beautiful amethyst. I haven't been able to identify the others yet. How would you like to go exploring on our day off from school next Friday?"

Bryce sounded the alarm. "Isn't that trespassing? It's fenced for a reason, you know."

"That's true, Bryce, but it's not posted with any signs. The wire fencing is rusty and the posts are falling down. The Bates Mine has been abandoned for years. Uncle Willie and Uncle Herbert always warned me that it was fenced to keep children out. We're not little kids; besides we have an assignment to complete."

"I'm game," responded Gordon.

"Me too," replied David.

"I'll think about it," frowned Bryce.

"One more thing." Curtis removed his gold-rimmed glasses. "While I was there, I went down quite a ways and discovered a wide ledge big enough for all of us to stand on. Below the ledge there was a huge hole. It was black as carbon. I threw some stones into it and could hear them bouncing at the bottom. I went back to the house and borrowed my uncle's flashlight. Guess what I saw when I shined the light from the ledge to the bottom?"

"Thirteen rattlesnakes," joked Gordon.

"No! A big tunnel. It went into the right side. This cave-in is over a mining tunnel that was used for the mining of iron ore."

Friday came and with it a blue-sky-day. It was the latter part of May. Robins were nest building, bees were buzzing on dandelions, and crows were cawing on the barn roof. One by one the four boys from Roosevelt School rode into the Anderson Farm on their bikes. It was mid-morning. Each boy had a rucksack containing lunch, favorite pop and a flashlight. David and Curtis also had about fifty feet of coiled rope.

After walking through the cow pasture, they moved onto an abandoned two-track. Finally they approached a grassy field arrayed with orange hawkeye. And there it was, the cave-in whose perimeter was fenced with rusty barbed wire.

"Okay, troopers, let's get on the other side and begin collecting."

With Curtis leading the way, Bryce, Gordon and David began collecting samples. The next couple of hours were filled with shouting as each discovered another unusual rock. Finally they reached the ledge and threw stones down trying to judge the distance to the bottom.

David took off his pack. "Let's eat! I'm starved."

After Curtis gave them the familiar pop bottle command they had used so frequently the summer at Spring Creek, they sat down to lunch.

"Boy, did my mom pack me a lunch and a half." Bryce laid out his banquet on a red bandanna. There were three sandwiches, a piece of apple pie, six chocolate chip cookies, an orange and two O'Henry candy bars.

Ham, chicken, meatloaf and egg sandwiches were exchanged in halves among the quartet of friends. Blueberries and peaches in small glass jars were eaten with gratitude to their mothers' canning skills. Bryce traded his apple pie with Gordon in exchange for his blueberries.

A cool draft came up from the wheelbarrow-sized hole adjacent to the ledge where the boys now rested.

Gordon emptied his pack with its collection of specimens. As he began counting, the others followed. "I've got thirteen of them," he said.

"You say you've got thirteen, Gordon. Are you sure they're not rattlesnakes?" teased Curtis.

Remembering his wisecrack earlier, Gordon's three companions made hissing sounds and poked their fingers into his ribs, making him giggle.

"Add them all up, Gordon," prodded Curtis. "I only have five."

"That makes thirty-five," replied Gordon.

Bryce reached down and picked up one as big as his fist. "I bet none of you have one like this."

He passed it around and David whistled. "Now this really looks like it has some gold in it. It sure is pretty looking quartz. What's the test for gold, Curtis?"

"Gold is soft," he replied. "Take your knife blade, Bryce, and scratch that gold looking stuff. "If it's not soft, the chances are it's fool's gold."

Bryce scraped the gold looking material. "It's hard. Must be fool's gold."

"I agree," commented Curtis. "It's probably pyrite. My grandpa Anderson was a diamond ore driller when he lived in Canada. This doesn't mean he drilled for diamonds, but that they used diamond bits on their drilling rigs. I have some samples at home. When he and his team would drill into the earth, they would bring up core samples. By examining each of them they could determine the type of rock or minerals that lay beneath. The core samples are actually a road map into the earth's crust."

Curtis reached into his pack and pulled out his olive colored military flashlight. "Get your flashlights and let's study this small cavern."

All four of them peered down. The beams reflected off the wet floor back onto the side walls, and slightly into the tunnel opening.

Broken timbers and debris were scattered about and totally blocking the opposite side of the tunnel.

Bryce coughed. "Sure is a cool breeze coming out of this hole. I wonder if this leads to the mine."

"Well, the Bates Mine is about three miles away." Curtis worked his flashlight beam back to the tunnel. "Look at that opening, it's really sculptured like that made by miners.

"My grandfather and uncle used to work in that mine. I remember when I used to play over at grandpa's house. I'd see them come home from work red as a beet. It was from working in all that red iron ore dust. They spent the whole day working underground.

"I had a habit of running back to the kitchen whenever I spotted the old black Dodge coming up the driveway. It was my habit to raid the lunch boxes for any goodies that were left. Grandpa enjoyed the canned fruit that grandma usually put in, but he didn't care for peaches. Boy, do I love peaches. I ate them right out of the small glass olive jar before grandma noticed."

"Let's measure the depth of this hole," suggested Bryce.

David took his fifty feet of rope and hurled the bulk of it to the bottom. "Looks like it's maybe thirty to forty feet," he observed.

"I sure wouldn't want to work in a cold, dark, wet mine," commented Gordon. "What would you do if you couldn't get out? What time is it, Curtis?"

"I have half past one o'clock," Curtis responded. "That's time enough to examine the tunnel and collect some more rocks."

"You're the knot expert, David. How about you taking your rope and tying it around that boulder next to the edge of this ledge. Remember this is our only lifeline out of here so tie a secure knot."

While David was busy anchoring the end of the rope to the boulder, Curtis took the other end and tied it around his waist.

He also looped the coil of rope he had brought around his left shoulder.

"Hey guys! Remember when we did that rope thing around the boulders a few years ago over on the Montreal River? Let's wear our packs down. Give me some light and I'll go check out the snake population for Gordon."

Holding the upper part of the rope in his right hand after looping it around his waist, he rejoined the other end and belayed downward. With feet against the ledge wall and flashlights illuminating the way, he slowly rapalled himself safely to the bottom.

"I'm down," he shouted back. "There's rope to spare. Looks like David was right. It's about forty feet. Gordon, you go next. David, since you're the heaviest, you go last."

Gordon and Bryce descended safely down the dark chamber.

David shouted, "Any snakes down there, Gordon? Here I come!"

Quickly he slid down the rope. "Too fast, David!" yelled Curtis. "Hold up a minute."

David stopped abruptly, and began swinging in the air. For some unknown reason he was not next to the wall of the opening. He was about ten feet above the outstretched arms of his companions.

In the blink of an eye, the boulder anchoring the rope rolled over the edge. There was a crashing deluge of debris falling downward with David slightly ahead of it.

"Look out!" Curtis shrieked. "Get his arms into the tunnel."

The flashlights had fallen to the ground streaking two beams of light in different directions. Suddenly, there was a high-pitched cracking sound like a twenty-two rifle being shot. The supporting beam at the tunnel's entrance splintered and fell on David's leg.

Choking with dust, David groaned. "I'm caught! Something's got my ankle. Don't pull! It hurts awful."

Picking up two of the flashlights, the boys took a large fragment of wood and pried the broken tamarack beam off from David's leg.

"Oh that feels better, but it still hurts. Where's my flashlight, guys?"

"Buried, my friend," spoke Curtis. "Where's yours, Gordon?"

"I dropped it when everything happened. It must have gone out."

Shining the two working lights about the area, they discovered it further in the tunnel.

Gordon picked it up. "It rattles when I shake it. It won't work. The glass and bulb are broken."

"Take mine," Bryce offered. "Let's look at David's leg." Bryce knelt down and examined David's right ankle. "No bone sticking out, so it's not a compound fracture. It's really red though, and there's something moving inside. I think we should make a splint for your leg and anchor it inside your shoe. You need to walk to get out of here, my friend."

"And how about a mud pack to keep the swelling down?" offered Curtis. "There's plenty of it on the floor of this tunnel."

"Yah. Let's get out of this snake pit." Gordon beamed the flashlight up into the opening only to discover that it was plugged with a jumble of rocks. "No way, guys. There's no light coming through and look at the size of the boulders. It would take a crane to move them. What are we going to do?"

Curtis removed his glasses and wiped them clean. The left lens was cracked on a diagonal. Shining his light into the tunnel, he said, "Looks like this is our only choice. Let's think this out before we do anything. What do we have to survive this debacle we're in?"

"De...who?" quipped Gordon. "Where did you get that word?"

"Our English teacher. It means a mess, that's what, Gordon. I thought I'd educate you a little."

"All right, teacher. We have our packs and two working flashlights."

"And we each have our pocket knives, and I have some of my lunch left," offered Bryce, "including my compass."

"This rope around my shoulder may prove helpful," concluded Curtis. "Keep your flashlight, Gordon, even if it doesn't work. We can use the batteries if one of ours goes out."

"What time is it, Curtis?" asked Gordon.

Taking out his pocket watch, he replied, "Three-thirty. Let's get moving, fellows. I sure don't want to stay in this dungeon of darkness overnight. You take my flashlight, Gordon, and lead the way. Bryce and I will support David between us. Let's use one flashlight and conserve the batteries just in case."

The tunnel was head high, and the foursome made their way slowly into the meandering maze. It was a dark, dusty and damp trail that seemed to zigzag continuously into endless blackness. The hours of afternoon disappeared into early evening. Progress was slow with David supported by his two friends and hopping on his left foot.

"I hear noise up ahead," Gordon announced. "It sounds like running water."

The group of displaced geologists halted. Sure enough, there was a sound of moving water. Up ahead, Gordon's flashlight caught the shimmer of water in its beam.

Bryce pointed his flashlight at the water's flow. "Would you look at that. It's a cascade of water coming down the tunnel wall. Look again. Here's a pool of water across our path and it seems to be emptying into a crevice."

"Sure does," remarked Curtis. "Let's stop here and rest for awhile. David can soak his foot. Taste the water and see if it's fit to drink."

Sure enough, the water was crystal clear.

"It tastes like spring water," announced Gordon.

"Great!" replied Curtis. "Let's fill our pop bottles after we've drunk enough. We can seal the tops with some scraps of wax paper from our packs. This is a real blessing.

"My grandpa's watch says it's seven-thirty. That means we've been walking for four hours. Maybe we've covered a mile. If it was three miles from Uncle Willie's house to the mine, than I kind of think there are two miles to go."

"How you doing, David?" asked Bryce as he removed the splint, shoe, and sock from David's foot. "It's swollen all right. Let's put it into the pool for awhile."

Curtis informed Gordon. "You take care of David for awhile. Bryce and I will take our flashlight and go further into the tunnel and do some exploring."

Walking through an iron mine tunnel wasn't so bad if it weren't for the darkness and cold, clammy air. Moving around the bend they had observed while standing by the running water, they came upon a junction of two tunnels.

"Which one should we take?" asked Bryce. "They're both the same size."

"Hmmm. You're left handed. Why don't we try that one first?"

Working their way forward, they noticed that the floor began to descend. A little later, they came into a large chamber. Scanning the walls with the light, it appeared that this was an area where the miners had stopped digging.

"Looks like they ran out of ore at this spot or had a cave-in." They scanned the room looking for a reason.

"There at the far end, Bryce. Look! The color of the rock wall is different. It's gray. Let's take a look.

"No red — it's dead," remarked Curtis. "This stuff is shale just like those flat pieces we first saw at our cave-in. So...they ran out of iron ore."

"Maybe we should spend the night here," offered Bryce. He beamed the light around the good sized room. "It sure would be a more roomy choice."

"It sure would. What was that pile of stuff your light just shined on?

Walking over to the corner next to the sheer shale wall, the two boys came upon a collection of mining junk in a heap. Sorting through it all they found a black mining lantern with a red globe, work coveralls and some wide flat boards.

"Let's see if there's any kerosene in the lantern," encouraged Curtis.

Bryce shook it and both of them heard the movement of liquid. Opening the screw cap, they peered through the hole with the flashlight beam.

"Looks like it's half full. It sure smells like kerosene. I've got matches in my Marble Match Safe. Let me light it and see if it still works."

"Hey! That's super! It reminds me of the light on a caboose." Curtis rubbed some of the dust off from the globe. "Let's go get the guys and spend the night here where it isn't so wet and confining."

It was nine o'clock when the four boys entered the chamber from the left tunnel. Bryce lit the kerosene lamp and a deep red glow permeated the miner's abandoned iron vein.

"It would be a good idea, Bryce, to take the globe off from the lantern. We would have more light. There's enough scrap wood over in that junk pile to make a little platform for each of us to sleep on," suggested Curtis.

Bryce and Gordon followed Curtis to the corner and began hauling the makeshift bed materials over to David.

Gordon piped up. "I think we can use those old mining jackets and overalls on top of the boards. It would help some from the cold."

"What do we have left for food, fellows?" asked Curtis.

Bryce laid out his red bandanna and the young men laid all the remaining eatables from their packs: one ham sandwich, two chocolate chip cookies, one candy bar, three pieces of Juicy Fruit Gum, one root beer barrel, three caramels, and crusts from Gordon's two sandwiches.

Gordon smacked his lips. "I'm starved, but there's nothing here to fill up on."

"You're right, my friend." Curtis took out his jackknife. "How about a four-way cut on the sandwich and we split the cookies in half? That way we each get a square meal. Get it guys, a square meal."

"That's what I'd call a square deal," spoke up David. "For dessert we can choose among the caramels and the root beer barrel."

"We'll save the rest for tomorrow," warned Curtis. "It would seem that we're about halfway so tomorrow night we should be out of here."

"And we have four bottles of water," interjected Bryce. "I think we should let David have the root beer barrel sort of for his pain."

With the abbreviated meal done, they tucked David in after putting another mud pack on his ankle. The tired and dusty group lay down on their board beds. All was darkness as never witnessed before. Far away in the tunnel, the echo of the falling water by the pool put them to sleep.

Somewhere in the blackness of their rock walled bedroom, a groan was heard. Curtis sat up. Nothing. Had he been dreaming? There it was again. *Oh, oh. It's David.* He turned on his flashlight and crawled over to his friend.

"David! David! What's the matter? Are you afraid?"

"Yes. It's the pain. It's so swollen and I have a terrible headache. Curtis, I think I'm dying. It's hard for me to breathe. This is a mine. Miners die in mine tunnels, because there isn't enough air. Isn't that true?"

Curtis placed his cold hand on David's forehead. It was hot.

"Listen to me, David. I'm going to give you some of my water to drink, but first I want to remind you of something. Remember when we were at the entrance to the cave-in sitting on the ledge. What was it we noticed about the air?"

"I...I remember now. There was a draft coming up out of the hole. I get it, Curtis. That means there was air coming up from the bottom, which had to be moving through the tunnel. And we're in the tunnel. Wow! What a relief. I was scared there just for a moment. Thanks a million. Before you go to sleep, would you pray for me?"

"Okay. Here's a prayer my mother taught me before I started school. 'Now I lay me down to sleep. I pray the Lord my soul to keep. If I should die before I wake, I pray thee Lord my soul to take. If I should live for other days, I pray thee Lord to keep my ways. Amen.' Now take a few swigs from my bottle and get some sleep."

Curtis returned to his plank bed, but now he was having a problem. No one knew he was claustrophobic. At sixteen years of age, his best buddies didn't know, neither did his parents. It was a secret known only to him.

There's something about being underground that makes you feel like the ceiling is caving in. It's oppressive. It's dark. There is no darkness like the darkness under ground. There is no fresh air. You take what there is into your lungs, but the air doesn't seem to go deep enough. You become afraid. It must be like drowning when all seems hopeless.

Breathe deeply, he told himself. *Get your mind on something else. Think about canoeing, ski jumping or Veronica. Quick, get the lantern and put the red globe on so it won't wake the others.*

The red glow of the miner's lantern was beautiful like the setting of the sun on Fortune Lake. *Now, hope and pray all of us get out of this calamity.*

The next day, there was no light to mark the morning. There was no breakfast. What little nourishment remained in their packs would be needed throughout the day. They drank some water, but Curtis had less.

They headed back to the junction of the two tunnels, and proceeded into the right hand one. Curtis did not take the lantern, because it had burned out while he was sleeping. It had been the remedy to his claustrophobia. He said nothing to the others, but wondered what another night would bring if they didn't reach the mine shaft today.

The morning of blackness took them through a route of curving and undulating carved out rock. In their packs they lugged that valuable cargo of specimens for science class. Gordon continued to light and lead the way with one flashlight. He had replaced the batteries with the ones he had saved. Curtis and Bryce persevered in supporting David who struggled with his hop-on-one-foot method. The swelling had not receded and the fever continued.

David spoke up, "Let's stop and rest for awhile, Gordon. We need something to eat and I need a drink of water."

Gordon focused the light on Curtis and asked, "What time is it, and how much farther do you think we have to walk before we get to the shaft?"

"Hey, how about that fellows. It's twelve o'clock noon right on the button."

Curtis returned the timepiece to his watch pocket and answered Gordon's question. "It's a slow pace we're walking, but we've walked all morning with some back-tracking. If we got in a mile yesterday, and another mile so far today, it looks like we should have a mile to go."

"That's super," exclaimed Bryce. "I've got an idea, guys. I forgot until last night, when we had the light of the lantern, that I brought my compass. Let's take a reading and see if we're heading south. In this dark tunnel we have no idea which way we're going. We know that the Bates Mine shaft is south from where we started. The compass should give us a direction in a matter of seconds."

"Wait just a minute, Bryce," spoke up Curtis. "Go ahead and try it, but remember what we learned while working on our orienteering merit badge in scouts. A compass is non-effective if the ground contains metal substances. Here we are with all kinds or iron ore tracings."

Bryce removed his pack, took out his dad's engineer's compass, and pointed it in the direction they were traveling. With Gordon's light on the dial, the needle pointed down instead of towards a compass point.

"You're right, Curtis. It's just like the manual said." 'A compass is totally unreliable in rock or soil containing iron or magnetite.'"

With the break over, and their dry iron-dusted tongues lubricated with a few swigs of water, Gordon flashed the beam down the tunnel.

"Hey, Gordon!" Curtis stopped abruptly with David holding on tightly. "What was that shiny reflection up ahead?"

They all saw it whatever it was. Some kind of metal was reflecting the light back towards them when it was at the right angle.

Gordon took some quick steps forward and then announced, "It's an ore car. It's on tracks."

"What do you know about that," grinned Bryce.

"Shine your light down the tracks, Gordon," instructed Curtis. "See if they're intact."

Sure enough. Rusty from age and dampness, the narrow tracks could be seen the length of the tunnel before them. Curtis took the other flashlight from his pack and shined it into the underground ore car. It was empty.

"David," he said. "I think you should be our guest and ride in style. All three of us will lift you up and in. You, my friend, are going to get a free ride. Bryce and I would rather push you on steel wheels than carry your one hundred forty pounds any further."

After the transfer of David to the ore car, they entered another chamber. It was much larger than the one they had slept in last night. Beaming both flashlights around this new miner's cavern, they discovered that this was some kind of ore car depot. Much to their chagrin, this place also had two tunnels leading out of it.

David stood up in his car. "There must be over twenty ore cars here. Now if only we had one of their engines."

"Time for celebration," announced Curtis. "Are you hungry, David? Let's dine on some of Gordon's left over bread crusts."

After the sparse snack of bread and a few more swigs of water, they had a meeting of the minds.

Shortly thereafter, they were pushing David's ore car ahead using the tunnel that proceeded on their right. The three boys rotated in pushing David as a tandem, thereby, giving one a rest. The noise of the steel wheels on the track was a welcome sound. Their spirits were bolstered by the day's discoveries. They had to be getting closer to the open shaft, yet they saw no light anywhere except the one beam from the friendly flashlight.

It was mid-afternoon and the ore car was moving so freely that it only required one pusher.

"Hey, fellows! Jump on the edge of the car and get a free ride like David. Gordon, you can stand on the front turnbuckle and be our headlight."

The minutes flew by as the foursome enjoyed their free ride. The speed was gradually increasing. Suddenly Gordon shouted, "There's no more track up ahead! We're going to crash!"

Off the tracks the car lurched forward churning up a cloud of iron ore dust as three of its riders went flying. David had been sleeping in the bottom of the car and now was yelling his head off.

Curtis picked himself up and retrieved the burning flashlight. After checking everyone over, they all agreed this was one close call.

David started laughing. "Look at the three of you. You are red with dust. Look at your faces. You look like men from Mars."

David's car had remained upright after it ran out of track. It was no easy chore, but they did get the car back onto the track. It was late afternoon when they returned to the car depot. Curtis, Bryce and Gordon were not only laden with red ore dust, but soaked with perspiration from the long hard push back.

Curtis looked at his watch. "It's five o'clock, guys, and we're bushed. What do you say we rest here for the night? I sure don't relish sleeping in a confining tunnel." He knew full well that another bout with his claustrophobia might lead to some kind of seizure if he slept in such oppressive confinement. There would be no lamp tonight.

Gordon responded angrily, "What do you mean, Curtis? It's always night here and I'm getting tired of it. You told us we should be getting out of here today. I don't see any shaft opening yet. Besides, my flashlight is so dim now it's turning orange."

"Cheer up, grumpy. Remember what I said earlier. We should have less than a mile to go to that mine shaft you're talking about. You can think as good as I can, Gordon. Figure it out for yourself."

Bryce joined in the conversation. "Let's hope this other spur of track isn't blocked like the one we crashed in."

David stood up in the ore car. "Curtis, we need to pray. You know how to better than any of us. We are in a jam and if that other tunnel is blocked than we have no way out of here. We're to young to die, and our thinking is limited to our own reasoning. Please do it now. We need help."

The four boys put their arms around each other's shoulders and Curtis prayed a prayer from the heart not a form prayer this time.

"I'm sorry I blew up, fellows," apologized Gordon. "I think some rest would do us all a favor. How's our water holding out?"

"You're our buddy, Gordon. Remember, we're all for one and one for all."

The dim light Gordon was holding went out. Curtis reached into his pack for the only working flashlight. A quick check of the pop bottles revealed only a few ounces left in each bottle. Curtis had barely a trickle.

"Let's rest for the night as best we can and get up early in the morning for a final push out from this dark underworld. Bryce, take a look at David's ankle and let's do another mud pack."

Examining David's ankle, he stated, "It's really swollen more and it's hot." He removed the splint and shoe.

Gordon pointed at the shoe. "What's that cigar looking thing by his foot?"

Bryce picked it up and wiped the dust off. "Well I'll be...it's a candle."

"And not only that, it's a plumbers candle," remarked Curtis. "That means it's a long burning one. They usually burn for six hours."

With the candle lit and David's ankle cared for, they shared the O'Henry candy bar four ways.

Curtis laid the pocket watch on an oily plank. It was ticking its way past seven o'clock.

"Look how that flame pulls to the left," remarked David. "I think the air even smells better here."

"It's a good sign," Curtis replied. "Remember what I said last night. As long as we can breathe, there's hope for tomorrow. Good night, fellows."

The candle burned for nearly six hours. Some time past midnight, the room resumed its blackness. The brain of Curtis seemed to sense the change, and the leader of this unforeseen expedition sat up suddenly breathing in short gasps. Tears came into his eyes and he prayed out loud.

"O Lord, please help me to breathe and be calm."

David was awake from his throbbing ankle. "What's the matter, Curtis?"

"I'm having trouble breathing, David."

"Turn your flashlight on. What time is it?"

"One o'clock, but we must save our last batteries. Here you take it."

"Listen to the ticking of the watch, Curtis. It sounds like our Big Ben Clock at home. It makes me feel safe."

Curtis laid his head down on his pack. It worked. The tick, tick, tick of the watch sounded like dripping water. His mind drifted back to the porch swing on his grandparents' farm. He could see his grandfather's calloused hands as they held this very watch he now possessed.

His grandfather Anderson spoke. "Someday when I'm gone, this watch will be yours. It's the most valuable possession I own next to my violin."

Thoughts about his grandfather and the beautiful marble clock on the mantle of his grandparent's home put Curtis into a dreaming slumber.

Hours later he awoke with a light shining on his face. "What is it, David?"

"I want to go home. Let's not wait. As long as we have strength, we should keep moving regardless of the time. Besides, down here there is no time. It's always night.

The watch hands pointed to the Roman Numerals five and twelve.

"You're right, David. Let's not tell the others what time it is. They won't know the difference anyway. Night — darkness, there is no day here. There's not even any morning. Man alive, if we didn't have this old watch, how would we ever tell what time it is?"

With David placed in a different ore car, the four comrades moved into the other tunnel. Gordon took the lead intermittently turning the flashlight on and off. They had to conserve the remaining two batteries. What was left in the glass pop bottles had been poured into David's.

Hours of labor turned their shirts into clinging dampness. The kicked up dust penetrated the dry throats. They were constantly coughing. Stomachs were crying for food as the energy of leg and arm muscles waited for deliverance from excruciating fatigue. Round and round went the steel wheels announcing the arrival of an ore car that hadn't appeared on this track in many years. Six o'clock moved to seven and seven to eight. The watch knew what the time was, but the struggle turned into exhausted plodding of three sets of smelly shoes. Now the watch kept track of the time. Nine o'clock, ten, eleven and finally noon.

David had some water. They shared the last of their rations: Juicy Fruit gum. There was enough for a half stick apiece, and that brought some fluid back into their mouths. Even the sweet smell buoyed their attitude.

Curtis sniffed. "I smell smoke! I may not be able to see very well, but my sense of smell makes up for it. I'm telling you guys, I smell smoke." He wiped his beaded brow with his red stained bandana.

Gordon lit up the tunnel ahead of them. "I feel a breeze, you guys."

With the gum and bathroom break over, the process of pushing began all over again. This time the tunnel track moved up a stiff incline.

"Gordon!" shouted Curtis. "We need you back here. It's too hard to push anymore."

"Hold on a minute," groaned Bryce. "My shirt is drenched. I'm going to take it off."

"Good idea, Bryce. I'll do likewise," replied Curtis.

Grunting, sweating, pushing, sometimes falling, the threesome committed their efforts to the forward movement of David's ore car. Within the hour, the track leveled off and the tunnel increased in size.

"I see daylight!" yelled Gordon, who was once again in the lead with the flashlight.

Chapter VI

The Old Iron Mine

The boys entered into a huge cavern of soft light. Looking upward and squinting with their necks tilted back as far as possible, they saw it. Beautiful daylight. Powder blue sky was patched like a quilt with cotton clouds. Flying above this chasm, a bald eagle circled directly over the mine shaft opening as a "welcome back to earth" greeting.

"Wow!" shouted David. "We made it. This has to be the shaft of the Bates Mine, don't you think?"

"Whew! Thank God." Bryce put his crimson streaked wet shirt back on. "We're saved and I am so glad to be alive to see just plain old daylight. Never again will I take for granted fresh air and living light."

Curtis leaned his chin on the thumb of his left hand deep in thought. "I agree, fellows. Life is a gift. This sure looks like the old mine shaft. Are we ever a long ways down this thing. It may be two hundred feet to the top. Mr. Mertz would say this is what science is all about; problem solving. Let's look around. Maybe Gordon can come up with another history lesson for getting us out of here. Remember the old raft we built on Spring Creek and his rollers idea."

"Yah," interrupted Gordon. "And remember it was Bryce's solution in getting the key logs out of that log jam. Let's give credit where credit is due."

Inspecting the base of the Bates Mine shaft revealed a massive timbered work bench. On top of it they discovered a long handled sledge hammer, two short handled ones, old stained coveralls, a can of Quaker State motor oil, a rusty kerosene lantern full of fuel, some claw hammers, wire cutters and a wrecking bar. Under the workbench was a three-legged milk stool, a five-gallon can half full of kerosene, some reels of steel cable and an empty galvanized pail.

Curtis pointed to several stacks of wooden boxes that had not been opened. "Now what do you imagine is in all of those containers, dynamite? Maybe the miners were afraid to take it out of here. Let's take a look."

Using two hammers, the tired, hungry, thirsty boys pried open the top of the rectangular box curious as to why so many were left at the bottom of the mine shaft.

"Look at that, will you," complained David. "Spikes! Short, steel spikes. Who would have believed it?"

"At least it isn't dynamite," Curtis replied. "Well, let's figure a way to get out of here."

With David sitting on the three legged stool, the quartet of school buddies studied the sidewalls of the mine shaft. Three of them were sheer.

"Look how different that one wall is cut," noted Curtis. "It's sort of shaped like a bluff for about three-quarters of the way up."

"And look at that small level spot way up there," Bryce observed.

Gordon bristled up his crew cut with his left hand. "Could it be that it's some kind of relay station in case there was trouble with the elevator they used?"

David asked, "But how would they get to that spot? It must be a hundred feet to that location."

They walked over to the curved wall while David sat on the old stool.

Curtis ran his hands over some of the rock wall. "I haven't a clue. There are no holes, cable guides, no ladder marks, nothing."

Gordon coughed. "We need water. My mouth is as dry as baking powder."

"Put a pebble in your mouth, Gordon," suggested Curtis. "Now it could be that they used some sort of pulley system. Let's take a break and rest for a while. We can give this some thought."

They took the boxes of spikes and laid them two abreast and long enough for a bed for each to have his own. In a matter of minutes the relief from fatigue while lying on their box beds, and glorying in the sunshine high above their heads put them to sleep.

Curtis fought the sleep trying to think of a solution to their dilemma. He was facing some of the small wooden boxes, which were loaded with about twenty-five spikes each. And there was the steel cable under the workbench. How could they use the cable to get out of there? And why were there so many small ore cars left in the mine tunnels? Maybe the cable broke or the elevator malfunctioned.

His mind wandered to the bluff shaped wall with its strange platform. *It's like a mountain. How do mountain climbers climb mountains?* And that was his last thought. Exhaustion, hunger and thirst put him to sleep.

Sometime later he awoke, walked over to the mysterious wall and examined it more closely. It was not hard igneous rock. This was shale. In their science class, they had learned that shale was a sedimentary rock. That meant it was a soft type of material.

Bryce awoke and came over. Their clothing stained red from their struggle with the dust and mud gave them the appearance of seasoned iron ore miners.

"Look here, Bryce." Curtis opened the long blade of his boy scout knife. He started scratching and pushing it into the facing of the wall. "It's sort of soft, you see. What do you know about mountain climbing?"

"Only what I've read from books and magazines. Mountain climbers use ropes and some kind of metal things to drive into cracks in the rock."

Gordon, hearing the voices, got up and joined in the discussion. "Hey, green eyes. How do mountaineers climb up steep mountains sort of like we have here?"

"That's easy," the history lover responded. "They lay down track like the railroad men."

"That's it exactly." Curtis beamed. He ran over to the workbench, picked up a steel spike and the small hand sledgehammer.

"Now, watch this. If this is really shale, it should go in fairly easy and hold this spike when I hammer it in."

Sure enough, With the spike driven into the rock wall it held firmly with a few inches remaining.

Bryce frowned. "You mean to say you want us to spike the wall all the way up to the top?" It's crazy, Curtis. One slip by any one of us and we wouldn't need to be rescued. We'd either die or be full of broken bones."

"Not so, Bryce. The whole face of this wall is curved inward all the way up to the ledge, or whatever that thing is up there."

"I agree." Gordon brushed back his blond crew-cut streaked with a deep tint of red. "Let's set up a plan."

It was mid-afternoon when the boys started working on their deliverance from the dungeon as they called it. Curtis, in spite of the cracked lens in his glasses, began the spiking process. The plan was to pound the spikes into the sloped face of the mine wall about every twelve inches. The curvature of the rock wall would keep the body with a slight forward lean. Once begun, the next boy under the spiker would remove a spike from his pack and hand it to the leader. Ten spikes was the maximum weight that one could carry safely without pulling the body backwards. When the ten spikes were pounded into the rock, the leaders would exchange places. It was decided that Gordon would be the pack carrier with Curtis and Bryce the spike setters.

David sat on the stool. The boys had surrounded him with boxes of spikes. In spite of the throbbing ankle, he counted out sets of ten spikes and placed them in the empty packs. He also tallied the number using a piece of iron ore which left a red streak when it was marked on a box.

For two hours they worked as a team. Ever so slowly, a ladder of spikes began to curl up the shale facing. David would also steer the leaders making sure the spike route didn't meander like some crawling snake.

Gordon sat down on an unopened box of spikes. "I'm done in, fellows. There's no more of me left."

It was nearly six o'clock. There was no water, no food, but looking up they had hope. Maybe someone would even come by today curious about all the pounding of steel on steel they had done. The May sun was setting and soon their hole in the ground would be in darkness. Back home their families would be sitting down to a spaghetti supper or maybe a meal of freshly baked pasties. The boys wondered where the search party was looking. There was no way they could find them underground unless they checked the cave-in site.

"Get your matches, Bryce. Let's see if that Hurricane Lantern has a good wick." Curtis put his damp shirt back on. "No more gloom and doom for us."

Bryce propped up David's ankle after an examination and applied another cold mud treatment.

David yawned. "You'd make a good doctor, Bryce. Maybe tomorrow we'll be out of here. What do you think, Curtis?"

"It looks to me that the ledge is as tall as a monarch white pine tree. That would make it close to one hundred fifty feet."

"Let's see," he responded. "If it's one hundred feet tall and we're inserting spikes every foot than that's one hundred spikes. Is that right?"

"You got it, David. And it's probably another thirty or forty feet to the top. I'm thinking they must have had a ladder of some sort. Hopefully it's still there."

"Okay. I got it. This afternoon we put in thirty spikes in three hours."

"That's ten spikes an hour, you guys," Bryce interrupted.

Gordon's snoring interrupted their calculations.

"He all tuckered out," said Curtis. "For a lightweight, he sure is a worker. And look at his face. He looks like Squanto."

"So...we need seventy more," David calculated. "Wow!

We could be out of here early tomorrow afternoon."

"Not so fast, David," warned Curtis. "The higher we go, the slower we go. It's going to be dangerous climbing back and forth. We will need more rest than ever and besides we're getting pretty weak. Let it go for now. We're all happy to be here with fresh air and an open window to our escape hatch. Let's turn in."

The lantern burned slowly through the darkness. At midnight, a stream of white light streaked down from a full moon. It bathed the boys with a blanket of peaceful sleep. On this night, David had no nightmare, and Curtis felt no oppression from his claustrophobia.

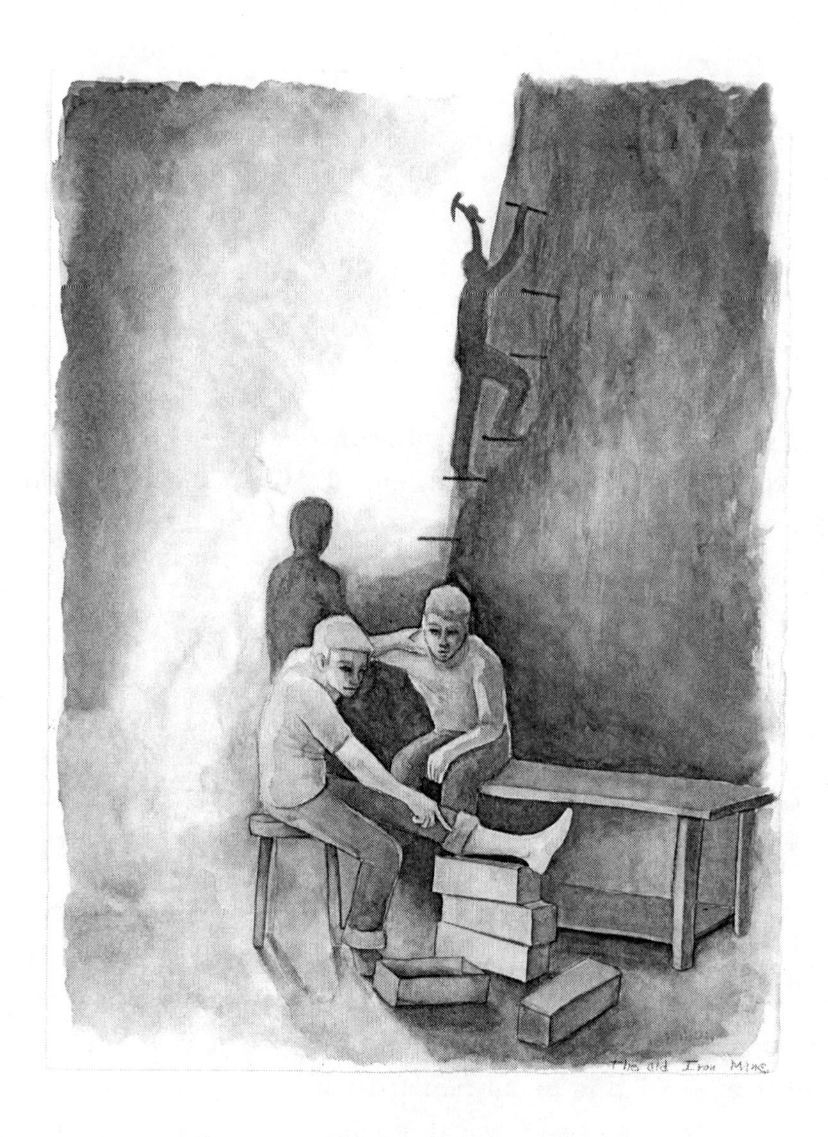
The old Iron Mine

A short while before dawn, a rumble overhead and a rifle shot sound echoed down the gunmetal gray of the mine shaft walls. Immediately a deluge of water from a thunderstorm came pouring down. In a panic, they picked up David and the lantern and crawled under the workbench.

The early morning cloudburst poured a pattern of raindrops over the floor of the mine shaft. A rivulet spurted off the platform high on the bluff wall.

"Quick!" shouted Curtis. "Get your pop bottles and I'll grab the pail. This is a Godsend."

The gushing waterfall filled the pop bottles in seconds and then the pail.

Gordon ran a bottle of water over to David. Moving a few wooden boxes under the workbench they drank their fill beyond reason.

They drank and drank and drank until they had drunk beyond caution. Now they were bloated. In short order, they realized they had satisfied their dehydration too quickly. Three of them ran for the far overhanging wall and emptied the contents of their stomachs.

David had drunk cautiously from his bottle and started laughing from his nest under the workbench.

"Hey, you all forgot the outdoor survival rule about moderation after a long absence from food or water. Oh, well, we sure got our money's worth."

The storm moved on. The warm spring rain felt wonderful on their red stained faces. The timepiece of Curtis told them that it was near sunrise. The kerosene lantern radiated out light and some warmth as they huddled around it.

"Now. If only we had some breakfast," Gordon pleaded. "Curtis, we are nearly out of here and I think we are so lucky. Maybe it's more than luck. Maybe God has spared our lives for some purpose. Would you pray? I need a prayer right now, because even this storm has given us the water we need to live."

Curtis prayed. "God in heaven. Thank you for sparing our lives and delivering us into daylight and fresh air. Help David's ankle to heal, and send us some food today. We are so hungry. Thank you in Christ's name. Amen."

As the sun began to warm the cold cavern that morning, a long vertical trail of spikes was visible to David. He tended to his job of filling the packs and coaching the route upward. Curtis and Bryce took turns pounding the steel spikes into the dark shale rock.

Gordon would reach back, remove a spike from his pack, and hand it to Curtis or Bryce. It would be carefully held on to the rock facing. The next step was to drive it more than halfway into the shale with the small sledge. This would never have worked, but for the inward slope of the bluff like shape they were traversing.

"Time for breakfast," Curtis shouted as he and Gordon descended.

David looked up and replied, "It's impressive, guys. We're a team just like in football. Each one of us does his part to move the ball ahead. I keep watching you fellows working higher and higher. I'm worried that with one false step we could lose one of you."

Curtis was tying a bandanna around his blistered right hand. "I know, I know, David. A couple of times my foot would slip on a wet spike and give me a scare. I'm thinking that from now on..."

Suddenly barking echoed off the mine shaft walls. All four looked up. Barely visible was a dog looking down at them and barking.

"He must have heard our pounding," responded Gordon. "Go get help, doggie," he yelled to the dog.

"I wonder if he's alone," said Bryce.

"Let's yell 'hello' on the count of three," suggested Curtis, "and see if anything happens."

After several attempts, nothing happened. Abruptly the dog left.

"Oh well, at least the dog knows we're here." David sighed.

"Let's see if we can make some sort of safety harness before we continue spiking," Curtis responded. "David's right. That height is just too dangerous to take chances."

"I'm thinking if we take and cut some of our rope into short lengths, we could tie one end around our belt. Then with the other end, we could hook it somehow to a spike near our shoulder. The problem is finding something to hook it to the spike."

Bryce walked over to the workbench and brought back a length of rusty cable. "Now look here," he said. "If we cut off a short piece, we can unwind the strands at each end. We can do the same for the loose end of the rope. By weaving the strands of the rope into the strands of the cable, we can make it work. The problem is how to cut the cable, and how to hook it to the spike."

Back to the workbench the trio rummaged around and found just the right hardware; snap swivels. With the wire cutters they measured out three lengths of cable. By loosening the strands of the steel cable, the boys were able to twist them into the round end of the swivel. Now all they had to do was snap it onto each spike as they made their ascent.

Up, up, up, the twosome climbed and labored with the ringing steel sounding like church bells on a Sunday morning. The calves of their legs were aching and the arch of each foot was sore to the bone.

Gordon complained to Curtis. "From now on, let's take a good rest after each descent. My feet are killing me."

The sun over head indicated it was about noon. "You're up to number seventy when you finish that pack," yelled David. "It looks like twenty more will put us near the ledge."

A short time later, David took a spike and hit it against a piece of pipe Bryce had scrounged up. "It's one o'clock. Time for chow. Come and get it."

They gathered around David's stool. "I made up a special brew for all of us. Remember when you gave me that root beer barrel, because you thought I needed some cheering up. I saved it. I crushed it up this morning and put some of the pieces in each of your water bottles. Take a swig."

Curtis wiped his mouth after taking a good drink.

"It sweetens the water. Thanks for the treat, David."

Gordon cocked his ear upward. "I hear barking. There's that dog again. Looks like maybe it's a collie."

In seconds there appeared a little girl beside the dog.

Curtis raised his voice. "We need help. Who are you?"

"What is ya fellas doin down dere? Did ya fall in? My name is Cyn-thi-a. Whose are ya and why ain't ya in school like my big sister?"

"We need help. Go get your mama or papa. Help us get out of here."

"Why doin ya jest climb up? I could reached down and help pull ya up. Does ya have a rope, cause I could tie it around the neck of Laddie here and he's strong like a horse and he could pull ya to the top. We could have a piknik. I got a piknik here in my bag and there's a peter bunter sandwich, cocoa chip cookies and a red dell swishious apple."

"She doesn't understand," warned Bryce. "If we keep talking to her she may slip and fall. We've got to get her away from the edge."

Curtis yelled back to the little girl. "Get back from the edge and lie down, Cynthia. No, don't sit down, lie down or you might fall in. There...that's better.

"Now listen to me, Cynthia. How old are you?"

"I'm almoas old enuff fer kinder school."

"That's a good little girl. We would like to buy your lunch. We will give you four quarters when we get out of here if we can have your picnic now."

"Four qwarters, wow! Ya betcha, mister. Here's my piknik."

The golden haired collie barked as the lunch in the brown paper bag descended with a smack on the rock floor of the mine shaft. It lay limp like a dead fish.

"Okay, fellas. Trow up my four qwarters."

"We can't, Cynthia. It's too high. Go get your folks. Help us out of here."

"I'm a goin, an I'm a gunna git another piknik for me self too."

Gordon flew to the paper bag along with Bryce and Curtis. Even David hobbled over. This was manna from heaven.

"Careful, Gordon," cautioned Curtis. "Bring it over to the workbench and let's see what's left."

Using the torn paper bag as a napkin, Gordon laid out four cut squares of a peanut butter and jelly sandwich, a big bruised red delicious apple, and wrapped in wax paper the crumbs from two large chocolate chip cookies.

"I told you so." David laughed. "Didn't I say it? Didn't I say 'Time for chow!' Don't you know I can smell food a mile away?"

"Look Gordon," interrupted Bryce, "there's no crusts on the bread. How about that. Maybe she's one of your long lost cousins."

"Listen here," he replied, "I promise before all the miners who ever worked in this mine, that I will forever eat my crusts. This is my vow."

"All right you starved, Roosevelt School, red faced, famished, iron ore miners," jested Curtis. "Let's eat, but save the cookie crumbs for supper."

After the wonderful lunch, Bryce and Gordon now ascended the steel pegs. Once more the ringing of steel on steel ricocheted in the mine chasm. They were now utilizing the new safety belt system.

While pounding spike number eighty-nine, a spike under the foot of Bryce broke loose hitting Gordon on the head. Bryce was partly hanging from his safety belt. His feet were dangling freely. Clang, the hand sledge rattled onto the stone floor. Holding onto one peg and grabbing another, Bryce clawed with his shoes onto two new footholds.

Gordon spoke with the sound of pain in his voice. "We need to get down quickly. My head is cut and I'm bleeding on my forehead. Release your harness, Bryce, and I'll guide your feet down to the safe pegs."

From below, Curtis shouted encouragement. "Don't look down. Continue to use your three point technique as you release from the one spike above you. You can make it if you take your time."

Both boys descended. Gordon had a trickle of blood from a cut on his head, and Bryce had a nasty laceration on his left arm.

Curtis washed their wounds with cold water. David tore his blue bandanna into pieces and covered their injuries.

"Eighty-nine in and this had to happen," complained Bryce.

"Thank God you're safe," uttered Curtis. "I think we need to call this a day. Maybe Cynthia will return with help soon. Did you get a good look at that platform on the ledge?"

Bryce sat down on a wooden box next to David. "It's an interesting place from what I could see. The platform is about twelve feet deep and covered with thick planking. It's much wider than that. There is an engine of some kind near the facing that goes up to the rim. I also saw a cable running from the machine up to a large wheel. Maybe it was some kind of hoist."

Curtis stood up and looked towards the platform and the opening.

"It obviously was some sort of hoist, Bryce. Could be it was used to maintain the elevator in some way. Do you think we could use the old cable to climb up to the top?"

"I couldn't tell if the cable was broken or not."

Curtis began moving toward the steel spike stairway. "I'm tempted to look at it right now. Looks like eleven more spikes will take us to the ledge."

Bryce's hands were shaking from the stress of his ordeal. "I'm all done, guys. I can't go up anymore. My head is dizzy and I've lost my confidence. Let's hope we're rescued."

David put his arm around the shoulders of Bryce. "That's all right, buddy. There's three of us injured now, and even Curtis has his own problems at night."

Cynthia was at the dining room table having supper along with her sister Jeanne, Mom and Dad. Her dolly was sitting next to her in a high chair.

"What did you do today, Cynthia?" asked her sister.

"Oh, I went hiking with Laddie. Mummy make me piknik."

"Did you see anything interesting?"

"Nope, cept fer four boys who weren't in school."

"Why weren't they in school?"

"Cause dey coon't get out of the hole."

Mother interrupted. "What hole, Cynthia? Don't tell me you went over to the Bates Mine. You know you're forbidden to even go close to that mine with all the cave-ins over there."

"I'm sorry, Mommy. Laddie ran away so I track him under da fence an over da big hole. An Mommy, I hear ringing noises so's I peek over to da edge an way down far away dare are four boys yelling at me an talking long time. Dey wan my piknik sack for four qwarters an dey say dey give me wen dey get out. Soooo...I throwd it don to dem."

Jeanne interrupted. "We are missing four boys from school, Mom and Dad. No one has seen them since Friday.

And here it is Monday and our school was just buzzing about their disappearance. They are in my science class. Could it be that Cynthia is telling the truth?"

"Jeanne, if the boys fell into that mine shaft they'd be dead. And you, Cynthia Kopenski, what did I tell you about making up fairy tales? If you are going to go to kindergarten, you must stop pretending with your dolly all the time. From now on you keep her away from this table."

"But Daddy, Laddie saw dem too."

"Not another word out of your mouth, young lady, or it's straight to bed."

After a supper of cookie crumbs and root beer flavored water, the tired team lay down on their box beds. Bryce and Gordon were both snoring in minutes.

In the friendly glare of the kerosene lamp, Curtis and David talked about the events of the day.

David spoke up, "Bryce told me the swelling has gone down some. I feel better today. My fever seems to be gone. I think all that water helped."

"That's splendid, David. I'm thinking about going up solo tomorrow."

"I'm all for it. You can tell by the eyes of Bryce that he's lost his confidence. And Gordon's complaining of being woozy. Wake me up when you decide to climb again and I'll spot for you."

At dawn's early light, Curtis was climbing slowly up the cold steel stakes. He replaced the missing spike Bryce slipped from, and began hammering the familiar steel on steel. Again, the clanging sound reverberated throughout the mine shaft and into the surrounding fields above. He had left his watch with David, who informed him he was averaging five minutes a spike. In an hour he should anchor in number one hundred.

That same morning, Cynthia's father had come out onto the porch to check on the weather and contemplate his work for the day. It was a quiet sunny day. The green grass was heavy with dew. Off in the distance, he could hear someone clanging away on steel. It was most likely his neighbor, Mr. Olson, repairing some of his machinery.

With the creaking of the screen door, Cynthia, appeared with her dolly.

"I'm sorry for da fussin last night, Daddy, an I din't sleep much also tinking of dem school boys down in dat long hole."

Mr. Kopenski remained silent. Cynthia cocked her head to the side and cupped her ear. "Dat's it, Daddy. Dem boys is hammerin agin. It's a ringin from over der where is da mine hole."

"Maybe you're telling the truth, Cynthia. Go get dressed. I'll get your mother and sister. We'll take a walk and see about this fable of yours."

The Kopenski family walked towards the abandoned Bates Mine and the sound of metal on metal. At the brink of the shaft, they saw Curtis pounding a spike. He did not notice the onlookers.

Jeanne whispered, "That boy looks like Curtis Anderson, but he's coated in red all over. He's in my science class, Dad."

"Let's not startle him. I can't believe what he's doing. Look at all those pegs beneath him. One false step and he's a gonner. I'll try a quick whistle."

Curtis looked up sideways. There on the rim he saw Cynthia and three others.

"Hey, Mr. school boy," she said. "Did ya eat my piknik?"

"We sure did, Cynthia. It was scrumptious. Oh, hi, Jeanne. Sure glad to see you. My friends are at the bottom and they're all injured. I'm so weak I feel sick to my stomach. I've been hoping to get to this platform. One more spike and I'll be able to climb onto it and rest."

"Curtis, there's all kinds of people looking for you fellows. What happened?"

"We got caught in a cave-in and we've been in all sorts of tunnels trying to get out of here."

"Curtis. I'm Mr. Kopenski. This is my family. We need to get you out of here. How serious are the injuries?"

"We think David has a broken ankle. He can only hobble. There's no way he can climb our spike stairway. Bryce has a deep cut on his arm. Gordon got hit on the head with a spike. He has a cut and is dizzy. Would you call our folks and tell them where to find us?"

"Will do, Curtis. My wife will call. Jeanne and Cynthia can keep you company. I'm heading for Mr. Olson's farm to get his tractor and lots of rope to get you all out of this thing. I'm thinking if we can make sort of a tire swing, we should be able to lift you boys out."

Curtis relayed all the news down to his buddies. He drove the last spike into the light colored shale and climbed onto the damp wooden platform. Gordon yelled up to his feminine audience and Curtis that he was going to make the climb.

News traveled fast on the party line as Mrs. Kopenski made calls to the boys' parents, the sheriff and Roosevelt School.

Within a half hour, Mr. Olson drove up with his gray Ford-Ferguson tractor. Mr. Kopenski rode on the rear hydraulic lift bar. He had brought a large tire and two coils of heavy rope. The tractor was backed up to a safe distance from the edge of the mine shaft. Each man took a coil of rope. They tied one end securely to the tow bar of the tractor. Finding the opposite end of the rope, both men tied it to the large truck tire.

By this time the sheriff and one of his deputies arrived. Parents were beginning to show up running to the unraveling spectacle.

The *Globe* newspaper hustled up with a photographer and reporter seeking details for a story.

There was a discussion among the sheriff, Mr. Kopenski, and Mr. Olson as to a plan which they all agreed on. This information was spoken to Curtis on the platform. He relayed the method of rescue to Bryce and David as Gordon continued his climb.

Sheriff Waite instructed Mr. Kopenski to provide the signals for the driver. Next, the sheriff and the deputy took hold of their coil of rope and began to lower the tire.

Curtis gave Gordon a final lift up to the platform. He was quivering all over from the strain of the climb. Looking down he said, "Can you believe this height, Curtis? What a project we accomplished."

Curtis interrupted his friend and yelled to the two at the bottom. "Get ready, David. The tire is coming down."

When it reached the bottom, Bryce helped David sit inside the large truck tire. And then he yelled, "Go ahead and lift."

The commands at the top were given. Mr. Olson slowly moved the tractor forward. Up, up, up came David. Due to an overhang of rock, the tire swing moved freely upward. As the tire approached the rim of the shaft, it appeared that David would be scraped against the overhang.

Sheriff Waite shouted to Mr. Kopenski, "Hold up the driver. David, you need to stand where you are sitting. Face the wall of the shaft. The tire is going to scrape against the rock overhang when it comes out. They'll help you as the tire creeps over the jagged edge."

David followed the instructions and slid on the tire holding tightly to the ropes. The crowd clapped their hands at his safe rescue. David was helped up, and limped over to his grandma.

As the tire swing descended towards Bryce, Gordon had made an interesting discovery. While Curtis was keeping tabs on the hoisting operation, he had been resting on his back watching the doings on at the ridge.

"Curtis, look over there for a minute. Is that a ladder? It must be made of steel. It has shades of the same rusty-gray color as the wall. No wonder none of us could see it. I wonder if it's too deteriorated to climb."

"Don't say anything. We'll give it a try when Bryce is safely on his way."

Bryce could see his two friends and waved as he went up. Curtis motioned with his arm and pointed to the ladder. Then he held his index finger to his lips as a gesture to keep quiet.

Rusty as it was, the truth is it had been anchored into the rock wall with long steel rods. If there is one thing that miners are skilled at it is drilling. These rods had to have been drilled in place. The boys climbed up the ladder and into a dilapidated shed.

Meanwhile, Bryce was safely ushered onto the sunny surface of the old Bates Iron Mine.

Now the eyes of the sheriff and his helpers moved to the platform where Curtis and Gordon were located.

Sheriff Waite shouted, "Where are you two?"

There was no answer.

"What are their names? Help me, someone."

Jeanne who had been standing with Cynthia during this whole rescue said, "Curtis and Gordon."

The sheriff yelled it out. "Curtis! Gordon! Where are you?"

The crowd now grew silent wondering if somehow there had been a tragedy at the platform. Had the two boys fallen into the bottom of the shaft?

Cynthia, in her curious cute way, had been looking up at a small knoll where an old tool shed stood. "Hey Mr. Share if," she giggled, "dere dey is. Whopee! Hare dey comb and dat tall one wit da glasses is da boss boy."

"We're over here!" Curtis yelled. The two boys came walking quickly towards the large gathering. Their families ran over to them with tears and expressions of joy.

Suddenly there was singing from a walking line of sophomores from Roosevelt School led by Mr. Mertz.

"For he's a jolly good fellow, for he's a jolly good fellow, for he's a jolly good fel—low, which nobody can deny."

"Well boys," Mr. Mertz began, "I didn't realize you were going to take your assignment of collecting specimens for science class so seriously. Your classmates are here to welcome you back to earth. Oh, by the way, did you get some good samples?"

Gordon bristled his reddish stained crew-cut back and reported. "Mr. Mertz, we got a total of thirty specimens, but there's just one problem. They're at the bottom of the mine shaft in our packs and we're just not going to go back down there in that prison and get them."

The newspaper photographer from the *Globe* came over and asked the boys for a shot with his camera. David took his familiar position supported between Bryce and Curtis. Gordon knelt down in front of the three and took a flashlight out from his pocket. The hair, faces, bare arms, hands and clothes of the four boys from Roosevelt School were deep red from their struggles with the old iron mine. To the crowd, they were images of miners from an era of the past.

Curtis interrupted the photographer. "Sir, could we have one more person in this picture? There's a little girl named Cynthia who found us two days ago. We bargained for her lunch promising four quarters if we could have it. She threw it down to us and it saved the day. We were starved and it revived our strength. Our conversation with her was like that with an angel sent from heaven.

She went home and told her family about us and here we are. She is our hero."

Cynthia walked out from her family with Dad nudging her forward.

"Mr. Curtis, what's a hair-o? Is it because mine is red on my head?"

"No, you sweet little girl. It doesn't mean your hair. It means someone who has done something very important. And that is you, our hero."

"Does dat mean I can get my four qwarters now?"

Curtis, Bryce, Gordon and David were laughing with tears washing down their stained cheeks. They reached into the watch pockets of their overalls and each took out a quarter and handed them to a smiling Cynthia. The photographer from the Ironwood newspaper took their picture.

Chapter VII

The French Bicycle

It was a lazy early summer afternoon. The sky was arrayed with its familiar white cumulus clouds. A warm wind from the southwest lofted the smell of freshly cut grass. The four boys from Roosevelt School were stretched out on the mowed lawn at the home of Curtis Anderson.

Their bicycles were lined up on the sidewalk leading to the front porch, ready for a moment's action. This was their style compared to other guys at school who would have laid them down on the ground. They got the idea from seeing pictures of the fighter planes at military airstrips. This had been during the early days of World War II. All four bikes had two different types of kickstands.

The lead bicycle was the pride of lanky, light brown- haired Curtis. The blue and ivory frame was highlighted with an abundance of chrome, handlebars, fenders, rims, light, and two shiny spring shock absorbers anchored to the front axle. The Monarch bicycle was a perfect match for its tall agile owner. They were both neat in appearance. Curtis kept it this way to draw attention away from his unusually thick glasses.

The next bike belonged to Bryce. It was an old green and white Roadmaster. Bryce had a swimmer's build and a Dutchman's blonde hair combed straight back. He lived nearest to Curtis.

David's red and white Columbia came third. It had a light mounted to the front fender like the others and a rear carrier with a large red reflector. Of the four boys, David was the strongest at arm wrestling. He also had the muscled stockiness of Bryce.

A gleaming new maroon and ivory trimmed Schwinn came last. Like the first bike, it too leaned on its newer designed side-mounted kickstand. The two older bikes had heavy rear kickstands that flipped up to a bracket at the end of the fender. This bicycle belonged to Gordon. He was sporting a crew cut. This haircut was beginning to be the style for some of the high school boys. Most of the older students from Ironwood had been in the war, and that was the way they had their hair cut. It really looked sharp.

The most striking feature of Gordon's bike was its large single chrome spring mounted to the front axle. Every bump was a call to action as the spring shock absorbed each depression on the road. Although it was the prettiest of all four, it was also the slowest. It was too heavy to be fast. Gordon came in last whenever they raced, but he enjoyed a comfortable ride.

"Hey, guys!" The voice of Curtis broke the bored silence. "Remember the raft we built at Spring Creek. Let's peddle out and take a look at the old creek. Maybe we can find that silver dollar that Bryce lost when we were building it."

The foursome jumped onto their bikes and were off to their old haunt. It was a four-mile trip. With a tailwind out of the southwest, they enjoyed the challenge of racing each other until they approached a huge hill. The climb up was difficult for their balloon-tired one-speed bikes. Near the top, a gravel road exited east into farming country.

"Looks like some commotion up ahead at the stop sign," yelled David.

All four boys climbed the hill in a standing position grunting to get enough pressure on the peddles to keep their bikes in motion. It was a long climb. Curtis was in the lead as usual. He enjoyed distance riding.

Gordon shouted, "It's a fight!"

They could see clearly now. There were four boys. Three of them were punching and kicking a tall boy wearing a white shirt and black pants. He was not fighting back, but trying to push them away. He kept using his shoulder to fend off the punches. Four bicycles were lying haphazardly on the gravel road.

Two of them finally grabbed the arms of the white-shirted one. A big kid in bib overalls and a white and black checkerboard shirt smacked him in the nose. They were all swearing at the tall black-haired fellow.

"Hit the freak again, Herman!" someone yelled.

Down onto the gravel road the young man fell.

"Blessed are the peacemakers," he declared.

The big brute named Herman spit in his face and shouted, "You religious nut! Why don't you go back to Ohio where you came from? We don't need no more sissy preachers around here. Those Baptist goody-goodies in town are bad enough."

Another boy with manure-caked shoes shrieked out, "And quit buying up our cow land. This country belongs to us heathen of the north."

The four panting riders on their bicycles neared the fight.

Gasping for breath, Curtis issued a command. "Leave him alone, or you'll get the same treatment, you cowards!"

The three antagonists quickly mounted their bikes, and off they flew towards town.

The four boys dismounted from their bikes and rushed over to the injured young fellow. Blood was running from his nose, blotching his white shirt. His pants were soiled with blood and dirt from the gravel road. His broad- brimmed, black hat was lying on the ground marked with footprints. Nearby lay his gold-rimmed glasses with one lens missing.

The boys took their clean handkerchiefs from their rear pockets and began wiping him clean. Bryce pinched the bleeding nose with his handkerchief to stop the bleeding.

"What happened?" inquired Curtis.

"Those three guys are the Carroll brothers. They've been swearing and teasing me ever since we moved up here last year from Ohio. We are Amish people, New Order Amish to be exact. I have no idea why they hate us. They own a farm somewhere between here and Bessemer."

"By the way, my name is Curtis Anderson. These are my best friends, Bryce, Gordon, and David. We live in town. I'm glad we came along when we did. Fighting is wrong. We were on our way to Spring Creek."

"I'm grateful for your rescue and help. My name is Luke Miller. Thank you for befriending me."

Picking up Luke's glasses and beginning to clean them, Curtis inquired, "Do you think you have any broken bones?"

Gordon interrupted, "Here's your lens next to these purple heal-all. I wouldn't have noticed it except it reflected the light back."

"Thanks, Gordon. It's expensive to replace. Oh, my! I sure am sore from all that kicking."

"Where do you live?" inquired Curtis.

"We're about a mile and a half east of here. My family has a dairy farm, and we make cheese to sell. It's the first place on the left."

"Do you think you can walk?" asked Curtis.

David and Bryce helped Luke to his feet. He began limping to his bike, which was not damaged.

"Hold on there, Luke," cautioned Curtis. "I'll get your bike, and you can use it for support. You're too shaky to ride."

"Hey, Luke!" smiled Gordon reaching into his pocket. "How about a piece of my favorite gum, Juicy Fruit?"

As the five boys walked their bikes towards the Miller farm, they talked about the upcoming activities of summer. This was the beginning of summer vacation from Roosevelt School. A barrage of questions descended upon the tall dark-haired boy with the strange black, broad- brimmed hat. They had never heard about Amish people before.

"How old are you?" questioned David.

"Seventeen," he responded.

Gordon stopped pushing his shiny Schwinn. "Why haven't we seen you in school?"

"We only go to school up to the eighth grade. We have our own schools. Since we're the only Amish up here, we do our schooling at home."

Curtis looked over at Luke's bicycle as they slowly walked the meandering gravel road. There was a British flag on the front label. The tires were skinny. It had a large rear hub and two hand brakes instead of a coaster brake. The bike was black, and the chain guard was entirely enclosed.

"Where did you get such a strange bicycle?" inquired Gordon.

"From my uncle," replied Luke. "He lived in Rhodesia for awhile."

David had a puzzled look on his face. "Why is the chain all covered up? We've taken ours apart many times in order to clean and lubricate it. Yours sure is different."

As Luke limped along pushing his English-made Raleigh bicycle, he told them about the dry dusty conditions in Rhodesia. "It used to be that the older exposed chain systems would collect all sorts of dirt and grime. Then the links would lock up. The English engineers solved this problem by enclosing the whole chain system. That kept it well oiled and dirt free.

"Moving parts, as you said, David, need oil," explained Luke. "The bicycle is a great invention, especially when you don't have a car."

"You seem to know a lot about bicycles," replied Bryce.

"Yup!" answered Luke. "The Amish don't drive automobiles or tractors. Our choices for transportation are horses, bicycles, or walking. On the farm, we have two plow horses, a couple of trotters to pull our buggies, and four bicycles. My uncle gave this one to me when he visited us in Ohio."

"Neat!" exclaimed Gordon. "How many are there in your family?"

"Twelve at last count," responded Luke. "There's Father, Mother, Leah, Jacob, Jeremiah, Ruth, Elizabeth, Matthew, Daniel, Rachel, Lydia, and myself. Isn't that a dozen?"

"Wow!" Curtis, who was almost six feet tall looked up at Luke who must have been two or three inches taller. "You've got us all beat. The four of us only have six brothers and sisters all together. Say, those are all Bible names. Any chance you're going to have a Mark or John?"

Everyone laughed. The group of walking bicyclists approached the gateway leading to the farm. Down in a gentle valley stood a two-story white house built on a small hill. A large red barn with its doors open was off to the southeast of the house. Scattered white and brown chickens were pecking at the ground. A windmill was spinning rapidly with its vane pointing northward. A small creek meandered between the entrance gate and the house. Over the creek was a small covered bridge built out of stones and dark wood. The boys were preoccupied with the panoramic scene. Curtis wondered if this brook could possibly be Spring Creek.

To the north, a large forest of maple and birch extended out from a large expanse of pasture. Hay fields dotted with large boulders and sporadic rock piles made up the scene to the west.

Far to the south, a weather-beaten barn stood solo in the middle of another hayfield. Three tall white pine trees stood next to it acting as sentinels. A small motionless windmill guarded a rubble of rocks near the old building.

Bryce and David pulled the bars at the entrance gate to the main farm and returned them to their slots as the group pushed their bicycles forward. Curtis and Luke led the parade down the driveway. A woman in a long, bright blue dress appeared on the porch. Beside her clung two little girls hanging onto her white apron.

When she observed Luke's limping walk, she immediately rushed upon him exclaiming, "What has happened to you, my son, and why are these strangers with you?"

After Luke's telling of the tale, there was a silence as each looked at the other. Father and six of the older children were out in the field stacking hay. Leah, who had remained at the house to help her mother with the chores, made an appearance after everyone had seated themselves on the porch.

"Come into the house and be seated at the table, boys. Leah will get you a snack. I want to examine and cleanse Luke's wounds."

A short time later, Curtis rose from his spindled chair and said, "Thank you, Mrs. Miller, for the biscuits, blackberry jam, and the milk. We best be going."

Leah, a year younger than Luke, looked at the foursome and said, "Maybe you will come again. What you did for my brother is our bond of friendship."

Gordon, with his light complexion and blonde crew cut, blushed as he looked at Leah and replied, "We sure would like to, wouldn't we, guys?"

"That's a splendid idea," spoke Mrs. Miller. "Then you can meet Father and the rest of our family. We don't have a phone. How about Sunday dinner a week from this Lord's Day. Check with your folks first, and maybe one of you could ride out here and let us know for sure."

Gordon rubbed his hand through his crew cut again and jumped up beside Curtis. "I'll do it in nothing flat. Maybe I can even give some of your children a ride on my new Schwinn."

Two weeks later, there were sixteen seated at the long pine table which was covered with an intricate designed crocheted table cloth.

Mr. Miller spoke. "Let us give thanks for our food.

"Father God, on this Lord's Day, we thank thee for the freedoms in our country. We thank thee for our health. We are grateful for the peace and joy that abides in our heart because our salvation rests in your Son, the Lord Jesus Christ. We appreciate the labor of Mother and the girls in preparing our meal. And finally, we thank thee for our four guests and the good Samaritan kindness they provided for our son, Luke. We pray this in Christ's name. Amen."

And everyone chorused another "Amen," except for Gordon and David as this was not their custom at meal time.

The gathering was dressed in their Sunday best. Mr. Miller and his boys wore tie-less white shirts and black pants. Curtis and his friends also wore white shirts, but with colorful ties. Their slacks were either blue or brown. Mrs. Miller and her five daughters wore long pastel-colored dresses.

All of the food on the long pine table was homemade.

"We raise and make most of our food," announced Mr. Miller. "Try some of our cheese. We make four different varieties. Later, we'll get Leah to show you our dairy shed."

The four guests focused their eyes momentarily on the tall girl with the long deep chestnut-colored hair. On the way home from their first meeting with the family, they had all agreed that she was prettier than any girl at Roosevelt School.

Curtis kept his own thoughts to himself. No girl could be as special as the girl from Wakefield, Veronica.

A loneliness swept over his soul. He hadn't seen her since the ski jumping competition two years ago.

Leah had been walking back and forth from the kitchen serving the gathering at the long table. She appeared tall with her long, wavy deep brown hair. Her simple full-length blue cotton dress was designed differently from that of her mother's. Her delicate features, natural pink cheeks, and green eyes made her appear like that of a porcelain doll.

When she finally sat down, the four guests looked at each other and knew that she was their equal if not more than that. She was shy, yet alert, intelligent, and graceful.

Curtis finally broke the silence of the meal. "Tell us, Mr. Miller, is it the food that makes you all so happy?"

"Well, that is partly the truth. It is the peace and joy we have through Christ that affects our countenance. After dinner, let us sit on the porch, and I will tell you of our journey through life and explain why we call ourselves New Order Amish."

"Leah," interjected Gordon, "who made the Dutch apple pie? It's my favorite."

Leah looked directly at Gordon. Her green eyes were almost a perfect match to his. "I made four of them yesterday. Mother has let me take over the pie making lately. This is the way we pass our skills down to the next family member. With Mother and Father teaching, we learn the correct way. I'm beginning to teach Ruth. Thank you for the kind words."

After dinner, Mr. Miller ushered all of the boys onto the front porch where there was a welcome breeze. The girls assisted Mrs. Miller with the kitchen tasks and some preparation for the evening meal.

"Mr. Miller, before you begin, my friends and I have been wondering why all of you wear so much black? I'm a Christian too, but the only ones I know of who wear black are men in the ministry; many pastors, Roman Catholic Priests, Sisters, and undertakers. Since God put color in the form of flowers and birds, we're curious as to the reason for the black."

"It is a good question, Curtis. Here is the reason for it. Color is an old science and has a long history. We trace our roots for this color to the early days of Christendom. The Roman Catholic priests wore black, Sisters of convents, and even undertakers as you say. It is a color that represents the subtraction of self in appearance.

"Like many men in the early ministry, we do not choose to bring attention to our personal appearance. Color would do this. The founders of our Christian association in the 1500's also believed that black would stand as a mark of religious distinction. Of course, it was readily available and less expensive than color. Remember, there was a time in history when only the nobles or rulers could wear certain colors such as purple and red.

"Curtis, you are quite right about your observations found in God's creation. And you have already observed that our women and girls do wear color. This is the way of the New Order Amish compared to that of the old order.

"Any questions, boys?

"And now for the story I promised you. When I was about your age, I got in trouble with my parents. The first time I went to a county fair one evening. This was considered worldly entertainment. Somehow my parents found out about it, confronted me, and I had to apologize to them and go before the men of the church and repent. This I did.

"The second time I got into trouble was for going to an evangelistic tent meeting. I was twenty-one years old at the time and still living at home. It was conducted by a man from Oklahoma. He preached the gospel from the Bible. He said the Bible declared all humans to be sinners. That Jesus Christ was the Son of God and came to save sinners—that we needed to repent from a sinful life and be born again by the Spirit of God.

"He told us we do not inherit a Christian life just because we're born in a Christian country or our group is Amish. No matter who or where we are, we need to have a personal relationship with Jesus Christ."

Gordon ran his hand again through his crew cut. "Mr. Miller, I'm not a Christian. Is becoming an Amish the same thing as becoming a Christian?"

"Absolutely not. Let me tell you boys something. No one but you knows whether or not you have a spiritual relationship with God through Jesus Christ. It gnaws at your soul day in and day out. I had no peace, no joy. I went to church, listened to the preaching, sang the songs, practiced the Amish way of life, but I was not a Christian.

"This preacher's message struck home to me. It was from the Bible, and I did not have what he taught the Bible said I should have. Then and there I asked God to forgive me of my sins, repented of my self-life, and accepted the sacrifice of Christ on the Cross for sin.

"Listen, boys, let me read it for you from the Scriptures. This is the book of Romans, chapter ten. 'If thou shalt confess with thy mouth the Lord Jesus, and shall believe in thine heart that God hath raised him from the dead, thou shalt be saved. For with the heart, man believeth unto righteousness; and with the mouth confession is made unto salvation.'

"Well, I left the Amish church. My parents, brothers, and sister shunned me. I became a part of the New Order Amish, which believes in salvation by grace. Eight years later I met my wife who had a similar experience and was searching for the truth.

"And here I am, forty-five years old, a family of ten children, a wonderful wife, and a great farm. We came here from Ohio so we could live in peace and have a fresh start away from relatives and being shunned."

Mr. Miller stopped the movement of his rocking chair, stood up on the porch, and looking at Luke said, "Take your friends on a tour of the farm. When you get back, I'll have Leah show them our little stone dairy shed."

Luke took them first to the big red barn. Here there were stalls for twenty Guernsey cows. It had an upper hayloft and various rooms for storage of vegetables and grain. An adjacent little barn was the shelter for the four horses and a few goats. It also had a hayloft.

They continued walking as Luke explained the function of the equipment shed, chicken coop, and root cellar. Finally they bypassed the large garden and entered the stone-faceted tool shop.

"Wow!" exclaimed David. "Could we have fun building things here."

"You even have a forge," observed Bryce. "We have a shop attached to our garage, but this is huge compared to ours."

"Remember, fellows," reminded Luke, "we do all of our repairs on this farm, and we even make some of our equipment."

Bryce tried pumping the large bellows. "I'm wondering why you don't have a lathe. Oh, yeah, I forgot, you don't have any electricity."

Curtis had been surveying the entire shop marveling like his friends at the array of tools and the different projects that could be worked on. He looked out a window and noticed the creek rushing past within a few feet of the building.

He called out to Luke. "Have you ever thought of putting in a waterwheel? With the creek so close, this would be a natural place for one."

"Would you believe it, Curtis; my father and I are working on a plan to do just that."

Outside again, the boys thanked Luke for the tour.

"Hey, Luke!" Gordon squinted into the sun. "There's one building you haven't shown us."

Pointing off to the west, there was an old bleached- out barn standing solo in a hay field. Three tall pine trees seemed out of place next to it.

"It's an old hay barn with a few stalls in it. My folks just bought another forty acres recently, and the barn came with it. Near as I can make out, it was an old farmstead. The house burned to the ground where you see that collection of stones. A hermit lived there. He was some World War I veteran who kept to himself. If you don't mind the walk, I'll take you down. There's something in the barn I'd like to show you."

As they walked towards the old hermit's place, Bryce remarked, "You sure have a picturesque place here, Luke. It's spacious, and you've a huge wood lot for firewood.

Any game around?"

"Sure is. We've got deer, partridge, rabbits, squirrels, and nice-sized brook trout down stream a bit. And then there's a big beaver colony and pond. That's where we really catch the big brookies."

Upon arriving, they entered through a side door of the windowless barn. The small rays of light entered through the open door. Before them, in the middle of the wooden floor was a rusty mower and a hay rake with a broken wheel. Worn horse bridles and other gear hung on wall pegs.

"Near as we can make out...."

Curtis began sneezing. "Sorry, Luke, it's my hay fever again. I'm good for about six of them before I get back to normal. Would you believe it, my record for sneezing is twelve."

"Wow! You must have it pretty bad. It seems like we all have some kind of ailment," replied Luke.

"We figure the old hermit was a veteran of World War I. We discovered some old uniforms and stuff left in a wooden box next to that first stall. Some yellow papers in it indicated that he had been in France. An old timer up the road apiece told us this man moved here about the same time he did, but he said the man wasn't social. When the house burned down from a lightning strike, the fellow moved on into town. He died shortly after that. He had no next of kin. We bought this old place from the bank.

"Come on over to this third stall. I want to show you something most unusual. I discovered it last week. It was covered with a piece of Army canvas."

All five of the boys crowded around the stall as Luke opened the creaky swinging door. Curtis sneezed again.

Before them stood a dusty-green bicycle. The handlebars were strange. They looked as though they had been bent downward into a curl at the ends. In fact, they looked more like ram's horns.

"Why that's a racing bike!" exclaimed Curtis. "Imagine that. I've never seen one before."

The leather, winding around the handlebars, was cracked and falling off. The brown leather saddle was deformed and decomposing.

Gordon whistled. "What in the world is that strange lever on the frame tube going down to the chain wheel?"

"That's a shifting lever," explained Curtis. "See how it goes all the way back to the rear wheel. I have a book at home about the Tour de France race, and this bike looks just like one of those."

"Let me take it outside, fellows," Luke insisted. "We can get a better look at her out there."

"Will you look at that now," observed Bryce. "It's got some kind of contraption on the rear axle. And look, I've never seen so many cogs before. All of our American bikes have only one, but this one has one, two, three, four, five of them. Well, I'll be a monkey's uncle."

"Holy mackerel!" chimed in David. "Is this some machine or ain't it? I mean *isn't* it. Look! It has not one, but two chainwheels."

As they continued gazing at the strange machine, they noted the flat, cracked, skinny tires. The chain was broken; it had no fenders, and most of the moving parts were caked with grease.

"Look at that frame. It doesn't have a speck of rust on it," noted Bryce. "The old hermit probably spent a lot of time polishing it. Boy! If only the bike could talk."

"The shifting lever is frozen up. Look, here, I can't get it to move," said Curtis.

Gordon dusted off the nameplate. "How about this, guys. It says, 'Made in France.'"

"By golly it does." David touched the pretty gold and silver plate with a lion's head emblazoned on it. "That old veteran must have brought it back from the war."

"And look again. It's the symbol for Peugeot!" exclaimed Curtis. "This is a world-class bicycle. I wonder how the old man got this thing anyway."

"What are you going to do with it?" asked Curtis.

"Restore it, Luke," piped up Gordon. "By the way, don't you think we should be getting back. I mean, Leah is supposed to take us on a tour of the dairy shed, and we don't want to be late."

"What's your hurry, Gordon? Which one is it you want to see, the dairy house or the guide?" teased David. "Next thing we know, you'll be back here tomorrow making cheese.

"There goes that hand again, right through the brush cut. I tell you, guys, he's as nervous as a cat."

"Yes, yes!" remarked Luke. "Let's do both. Go up and see Leah and restore the bicycle. I'll ask my father if we can bring it up to the shop and rebuild the whole thing."

Curtis put his arm around Luke. "It's such a unique bike. We'd all be glad to help you. I can write to France using my dad's new Royal typewriter and see about getting the parts we need."

Back at the house, the family was resting as was their Sunday custom. Leah was swinging on the front porch.

While the four boys toured the dairy shed, Luke went into the house to talk to his father about the bicycle restoration project.

Gordon kept Leah busy with many questions about making cheese.

Luke returned to the little creamery smiling. "It's fine with my father, but my daily work on the farm must be done first. Of course, we don't work on the Lord's Day."

The boys gave each other the familiar fist tap on the upper arm muscle and grinned in pleasure with the news.

Curtis took off his heavy glasses. Wiping them clean with a handkerchief, he beckoned to Luke. "I've got an idea. How about Bryce, Gordon, David, and myself helping you with your work. Whatever time we contribute to your chores will cut down on the length of time it takes you to do them. That would free all of us to work on the bike. In fact, we could come out some days and work, and you might get nearly a whole day off occasionally. We would learn something about farming, and together we could restore the Peugeot."

It was near the time of the summer solstice before they began the dismantling of the racing bike. Twice each week, four bicyclists could be seen climbing the long hill north of town and whizzing out to the Miller farm. The three high school hoodlums who beat up Luke were nowhere to be found. Tuesday and Wednesdays were the farm workdays for the quartet from Ironwood. Thursday afternoons were set aside for working in the shop on the bicycle.

Each boy had a job that matched his abilities. Luke was the general overseer. Curtis was the foreman with his organizational skills and knowledge. Bryce did the sketch work indicating the placement of all the parts. David was an excellent mechanic and did much of the dismantling, although they all contributed from time to time. Gordon, with his meticulous note-taking skills, labeled each part with tags. Luke gathered them into containers and placed them on shelves.

"Have you noticed that none of the bearings are encased in a retainer like our bikes. Every bearing is loose, so they're free floating." David wiped the grease from his chin. "I've never seen so many bearings in all my life for just one bike."

"I figure it will take a month before we get the parts from France," announced Curtis. "We've been nearly two weeks on this project, and I just air mailed Gordon's list out last Friday. Hopefully, the parts will come by air to New York and then by train to Ironwood. If they have everything in stock, maybe earlier. I wonder what kind of a story they will have to tell us about this unusual relic."

List of Replacement Parts:

1 brooks leather saddle
2 rolls handlebar tape
6 chain links
1 chain tool
16 crankshaft bearings
2 crankshaft cups
16 front hub bearings
1 shifting lever
1 derailleur
32 rear hub bearings
12 upper and lower race bearings
4 fork races
3 allen wrenches
3 brake cables
3 brake blocks
3 shifting cables
3 brake cables

By the fourth of July, the first cutting of hay was in the barn. New jobs on the farm now included weeding the garden, picking strawberries and raspberries, spraying the fruit trees, and cultivating long rows of potatoes and rutabagas.

On the final afternoon of cleaning up the old green Peugeot, the five boys were sitting on two pine benches in the shop. The discussion they were having centered on what Luke was going to do with the bike once it was reassembled.

The door was open to a cool breeze. Someone outside yelled, "I won!" In through the doorway came young Matthew and Daniel. Looking up towards a ceiling beam, they noticed the suspended frame of the bright green bicycle. It was barren of all of its parts.

"Look at that!" shouted Daniel. "They've destroyed the war bike."

Pointing towards the diamond-shaped frame, Matthew exclaimed, "Why are you ruining that racing bike?"

Luke reached up and took the bicycle skeleton down from the two ropes holding it to the beam.

"Curtis," he said, "explain to these two little brothers of mine why we've stripped it down to its frame."

Curtis took the frame from Luke. Opening a vice on the worktable he placed it right side up into the vice taking care to protect the frame from being scratched with two pieces of wood.

"Okay, Matthew and Daniel, listen carefully. I'm going to give you a lesson on bicycle building. A bicycle begins with the shape of a triangle. This gives it strength. These long pieces are called tubes and are made of lightweight steel.

"Now, in order to put the tubes together, they need to be fastened. Look here. Do you see these special designed short pieces? They are called lugs. These are even painted red for decoration. The end of the tubes slide through these hollow lugs. Using a torch, they are welded together. The welders call it brazing.

"How many metal tubes do you count, boys?"

"Three," they responded.

"That's almost right. Look again. There are four tubes.

"How many lugs do you see?"

"Six," they chorused.

"Right! You got it this time.

"Now let's look at the front of the frame. Here we have a short hollow piece open at both ends. It's a small tube, and it's easy to miss. This is called the head tube.

"Now here's a separate piece with two long tubes that come together forming one at the top. This is called the fork. The fork will hold the wheel and the handlebars to the bike."

Luke handed Curtis the green fork from a nearby shelf. Next he handed him the front rim. He fastened it to the fork. "Watch what I do with the fork." Carefully he pushed it through the short head tube.

"Oh, I see," grinned Daniel, "but how do you get it to stay there without falling out?"

"Good question. Now let me ask you boys a question. What would happen if we bolted it on the bike like it is?"

"I think I know," answered Matthew. "The wheel wouldn't turn. It would be locked tight, and the bike would go straight ahead."

"Exactly!" Curtis patted him on the back. "Maybe you two can watch us reassemble the bike. Let me show you another mystery of this bicycle.

"David, hand me the old races for the fork.

"Look, boys. These two pieces sort of look like thick washers. See how each has a groove. These are called races. Now watch as I take the fork out of the head tube. I take this race and slide it down over the top of the fork part. Now, the bearings will go all around the race being held in place with grease. I put the other race into the bottom of the head tube, push the two together, and 'voilla.' Now, what happens to the fork?"

"I see, I see," shouted Daniel. "It will turn like Mom's rolling pin."

"That's right. We use grease to hold the bearings in place, and it also helps it to turn more easily. All of the moving parts of the bike work using some system of bearings. Come back when we get our parts in from France, and you can watch."

"Mr. Curtis," inquired Matthew, "what does 'vanilla' mean?"

"Vanilla! No, no! It's 'voilla,' and it's the French word for 'good.'"

"School's out!" Leah stood at the door. For the first time Curtis noticed she bore a strong resemblance to Veronica. "I've been listening and learning too. You're a good teacher, Curtis."

"Leah! I smell chocolate chip cookies," grinned Gordon. "Did you bake this afternoon just for us?"

"Come on, fellows. You, too, Matthew and Daniel. Cookies and milk are on the table." Leah, wearing a long aqua cotton dress, led the way.

It was like a birthday party. The Miller family and the four boys from Roosevelt school were gathered around the large workbench in the shop. In the middle sat a box wrapped in brown paper tied with heavy white cord. Multiple French stamps adorned the upper right-hand corner. It was a warm evening in early August. Everyone had enjoyed a special celebration, dinner of fried chicken and fresh blueberry pie.

"You can have the honors, Luke," announced Curtis. "Check the items off, Gordon, as soon as Luke identifies each one."

Necks stretched from different directions as the gathering of sixteen observed the unpacking and identification of the French bike's parts.

"Look at that beautiful new Campagnolo derailleur," beamed Bryce.

Luke handed it to him to pass around.

"It looks like a can opener," blurted out little Lydia.

Half an hour later the box was empty. "Everything's here according to our checklist," declared Gordon.

"This derailleur mechanism is really a mystery to us. As much as we know about bicycles, we've never come across one of these before. I'd like Gordon to read the letter from Peugeot explaining how this intriguing part works."

After the letter of explanation, Mr. Miller stroked his beard. "It's time to clear the room, family. The moment of truth has arrived for our mechanics to plan how they're going to put this friendly relic back together again. Perhaps tomorrow morning would be a better time to work on it, boys, when your thinking is clear."

The following day was an unusually cold one for summer. Luke had prepared a fire in the shop stove.

Curtis and Luke had the most experience working on bicycles; therefore, Curtis coordinated the information from Bryce's diagrams and Gordon's checklist. Luke and David assisted each other using the special metric tools the Peugeot company included at no extra charge for the assembly.

Curtis took the fork and handed it to Luke. "Let's do the headset first. One of you needs to be the grease monkey, and the other needs to keep his hands clean for the assembly."

The frame was carefully placed back into the vice with the handmade wooden blocks to protect the green-painted surface. Having it upside down made for a convenient work position.

First the fork was installed with its many bearings stuck in grease to keep them from falling out. "Hold off on the handlebars," cautioned Curtis. "This would be easier with the bike upright."

Next came the crank set——more new bearings, grease, and assembly. When that was finished, the key to the rebuilt bike would be the bolting on of the new derailleur. One bolt took care of this.

"Gordon, why don't you and Bryce put the new tubes and tires on the two aluminum rims. Be careful about pinching the tubes. Put a little air in them first."

Shortly thereafter, the chain and wheels were installed. Luke removed the Peugeot from the vice, and the boys attached the stem, handlebars, seat post, and seat.

"Whew! There sure is a lot to building a racing bike."

It was approaching lunchtime when in came Matthew and Daniel. "Mother says lunch will...wow! Look at that! It's a bicycle again."

"All that's left is the brake and shifting cables. Oh, yah, the handlebar tape, too," replied David with the two rolls in his hand.

"What's for lunch?" inquired Gordon.

"Pasties!" chorused the two onlookers. "Mom has just learned how to make this special food the iron miners like to eat."

After lunch, the finishing touches were completed to the bike. Everyone assembled outside the shop as Luke brought out the sleek green and red Peugeot with its shiny silver alloy parts.

Curtis spoke up. "This work has been the partnership of five of us, and everyone here has been an encouragement in this project. We are happy beyond words for your hospitality and friendship. We think the maiden voyage should go to Luke, the owner of the war bike."

Up on the saddle and down the road Luke flew shifting gears as he went towards the covered bridge. He disappeared down the main road returning a short time later breathing heavily.

"It's super fast, and you've got to watch it on the loose gravel, or you'll lose control," cautioned Luke.

Next, the four boys took their turns. When Curtis finished his ride, he walked the bike over to Leah. "You try it, young lady. With all those great snacks you made for us, you deserve a special privilege. There's not a girl for miles around who has ever ridden a ten-speed racer like this."

"Thank you," she said, "but with my long dress you'd have to cut the top tube off before I could get on. I appreciate the thought."

After the family disbanded, the boys' conversation switched to a better place to ride.

"What we really need is a training track," remarked David.

"Right!" replied Bryce.

"How about the abandoned runway at old Camp Norrie?" suggested Gordon. "That has a macadam surface."

Curtis pushed the bike over to Luke. "What do you think?"

"Let me check with Father first."

During the afternoon, the five of them took turns riding down the runway. A few adjustments were made to fine-tune the derailleur as well. Finally, Curtis said, "Let's do a time trial. I've got a pocket watch with a second hand on it, and so does Bryce. We'll have a watch at each end and record the times. To be fair, let's raise our hand with a handkerchief and drop the hand quickly to start. I doubt we will be able to hear a signal."

After four time trials apiece, they reassembled.

Gordon calculated the times and announced, "And the winner of three out of four heats is...bugles please."

Each schoolmate put his hands together with the knuckles touching, thumbs side by side, and blowing through a small hole that was formed made a bugle-like sound. "And the winner of the Tour de France time trial is...more bugles please...Luke Miller. Curtis Anderson won the last heat, but Luke on the green Peugeot won the first three."

As the red-faced quintet rode back to the farm, there was incessant talk about the racing bike and the advantage of shifting gears.

"Can we come out and race it sometime?" asked Curtis. "It looks like our mission is finished. We would still like to help out on the farm, and I know Gordon has become attached to Leah's cookies."

With the restoration of the racing bike complete, the Miller family invited the boys out for their second Sunday dinner.

Chapter VIII

Circle of Friends

The second Sunday dinner for the four boys from Roosevelt School was equal to that of their first, but this one was different in many ways. Now they were intimate friends with the whole Miller family and especially their eldest son, Luke.

After a hearty roast beef meal with a peach cobbler dessert, Mr. Miller spoke up. "What would you boys like to discuss this time?"

Gordon brushed his hair back with his right hand. "Tell us why baptism is so important to the Amish?"

They adjourned from the familiar lace-covered dining room table to the living room. Mrs. Miller and some of the younger girls busied themselves in the kitchen while the rest of the dinner party seated themselves on an array of homemade pine furniture.

Mr. Miller responded to Gordon's question. "Why, of course, Jesus Christ was baptized. That really should be enough if we are to be followers of his teachings. And he was baptized by John the Baptist in the Jordan River as it was the custom of John to baptize by immersion."

Both Gordon and David looked puzzled.

"Yes," said Gordon, "but in Bryce's church they baptize babies. Then in the church where Curtis goes they only baptize those old enough to be called believers."

"That's right," Curtis interjected. "And we baptize by immersion not sprinkling someone's head. We are anabaptists like the Amish and Mennonites, except we baptize by immersion. Why do the Amish baptize like the Methodists?"

"Whoa, boys! So many questions all at once. One correction, Curtis. We do not baptize by sprinkling, and we don't baptize babies. We use a pitcher and pour water over a believer's head. Now, let's return to the first question."

"I've never been baptized either way," interrupted Gordon.

"Back to your question, Gordon." Reaching for his Bible, Mr. Miller smiled and said, "We need the Bible and history to answer this question. Baptism is important to all Christians; however, it does not make you a Christian anymore than wearing a wedding band makes you a husband.

"Leah, get your Bible and read the place in the Gospel of Matthew where it first mentions baptism. I think its chapter three."

Leah read from chapter three, verses one, two and thirteen through sixteen.

> "'In those days came John the Baptist, preaching in the wilderness of Judea. And saying, Repent ye: for the, kingdom of heaven is at hand.'"
>
> "Then cometh Jesus from Galilee to Jordan unto John, to be baptized of him. But John forbade him, saying, 'I have need to be baptized of thee, and

> comest thou to me?' And Jesus answering said unto him, 'Suffer it to be so now: for thus it becometh us to fulfill all righteousness.' Then he suffered him. And Jesus when he was baptized, went up straightway out of the water: and lo, the heavens were opened unto him, and he saw the Spirit of God descending like a dove and lighting upon him. And lo a voice from heaven, saying, 'This is my beloved Son, in whom I am well pleased.'"

"Is it not clear, Gordon? John the Baptist baptized people in the river Jordan, but he told them first they must repent.

Can anyone tell us what repentance means?"

Many hands were raised.

"Jeremiah, you tell us."

"Father, it means to change the direction you are going in and to follow a different way."

"That's it exactly," commended his father. "In fact, before the followers of Jesus were called Christians at a place called Antioch, they were called 'Followers of the Way.' What way? A new way."

Gordon raised his hand. "So, if I'm baptized, I'm a follower of the *way*?"

"Not true," interrupted Curtis. "Mr. Miller said, 'Wearing a wedding band doesn't make you a husband.' There is a condition before marriage just as there is before baptism."

"Correct again, Curtis," complimented Mr. Miller. "Love or some kind of agreement occurs before a marriage, and repentance comes before baptism."

David was sitting on a long padded bench next to Gordon. David felt Gordon's muscles suddenly tense in his right arm. He knew that his friend was about to run his hand through his hair again. David pushed down on Gordon's hand. Gordon jerked his hand towards his crew cut, but it wouldn't move.

"Gotcha this time," joked David.

"Oh, I see," exclaimed Gordon who subtly pushed his shoe onto David's. "But what is repentance again?"

"Just what Jeremiah said," asserted Mr. Miller. "When you repent, you're really changing your mind about your *self* and the direction you are going. You perceive that something is wrong in your life, and you want it changed. You desire to follow a new way. That new way is the *way* of Christ. Remember what I told you about my search a few weeks ago."

"And what is the *way* of Christ?" asked Gordon.

Mr. Miller took the family Bible from his lap and opened it to Matthew 16:24. "Here, Gordon. You have a seeking spirit. Read verse twenty-four out loud."

"'Then,' said Jesus unto his disciples, 'If any man will come after me, let him deny himself, and take up his cross, and follow me.'"

"See the words 'deny himself' and 'follow me.' Followers of Jesus believe he is the Son of God and that the whole human race is separated from God because of sin. Jesus Christ came into this world from his home in heaven to provide for a salvation in which a person could have a spiritual relationship with God. You don't automatically have one. Each person needs to repent of sin and self and act on the Gospel. Christ, the God-Man, died for all and provided the *way*. When you are willing to repent and receive God into your life, this brings into your life a new spiritual birth. Each one of us needs to trust Him for a new *way* of life, or to be born of the Spirit.

"Listen to another verse from the Scriptures that makes it so clear. 'Being born again, not of corruptible seed, but by the Word of God, which liveth and abideth forever.'"

Mrs. Miller had returned from the kitchen and was sitting in her rocker listening to the dialogue.

"Why do we have Christmas and Easter?" she asked the four guests. "I have to admit the emphasis today is more on celebrating than on the meaning of the actual events."

"Well, it's a holiday off from school," replied David.

"But, David, for some of us it's a time to remember the birth, death, and resurrection of Jesus Christ," responded Curtis. "I believe the birth of Christ was a supernatural event. There was no man involved in the conception of Jesus. This made him sinless because the Holy Spirit of God worked in the body of Mary. Jesus Christ was holy in heaven and holy on Earth."

"That's so." Luke opened his Bible to the book of his namesake and read from chapter one, verses 26-35. "This should also be included in the Christmas story because it shows how it all happened from the start."

"Even Mary needed a savior," responded Leah.

Luke read verse forty-seven. "'And my spirit hath rejoiced in God my Savior.'"

Mrs. Miller continued the discussion. "Has anyone ever wondered why Mary needed a savior?"

Curtis took off his thick-lensed glasses, wiping the oil from its nosepiece. He responded to the question from a truth he had learned from his pastor. "She had a mother and father just like us; therefore, she had to have been born with a sinful nature."

"Exactly!" agreed Mrs. Miller. "She was probably the age of Leah when she conceived."

Leah blushed. She took a quick look at Gordon and David. Then she spoke up. "It's a shame that Easter is more about eggs and bunnies in your school than historical truth. Listen as I read for you the whole truth about Easter from the Gospel of John, chapters nineteen and twenty."

Tears fell from her green eyes as she felt the physical pain at the crucifixion of Jesus Christ, the God-Man.

"Let me finish the verses for you," interceded Luke for his sister. "And now, listen to my favorite verse in the Bible. It's John 11:25 and 26.

"...I am the resurrection and the life: he that believeth in me, though he were dead, yet shall he live. And whosoever liveth and believeth in me shall never die."

Mr. Miller stroked his gray beard. "You see, the human race is dead spiritually and needs a new birth. When we truly repent and believe on Christ as the Son of God, we begin to live in the Spirit for the first time in our life. He cleanses our spirit by giving us the Holy Spirit."

All was strangely quiet. The ticking of the marble clock on the buffet was interrupted with the chiming of four o'clock.

Bryce looked around the room observing a most unusual scene. All of the Miller family had a Bible on their lap except for the two little girls who had fallen asleep near their mother's rocker. "You folks are most serious about your religion, and I admire you."

"Thank you," replied Mr. Miller. "But remember this, being a Christian is not a religion you practice like other religions. It is a life-changing experience you live. It's like your blood. It flows in you all the time. It's nourishment for your spirit like blood is for your body."

Curtis stood up. "I can remember a time in a country church near my grandparents' farm near Iron River when I repented of my sin and self-life and trusted Christ as my Savior and Lord. The Bible speaks it better than I: 'If anyone be in Christ, he is a new creation. Old things are passed away; behold all things are become new.'"

Mr. Miller stood up from his rocker, walked over to Curtis, and put his arm around his shoulders. "Perhaps you will be a minister someday. It takes courage to speak the truth in front of others."

The gentle father of the Miller family was a short man who was prematurely balding through the center of his hair. The gleam in his eyes and his friendly disposition tended to disarm any antagonism by those of a differing attitude. You could sense his love and devotion to Christ.

Gordon had been deeply moved by the Scriptures and the comments of the Miller family. Now he stood and joined Mr. Miller and Curtis. He had grown taller during these summer months, and he was letting his crew cut grow out.

He spoke softly. "I almost believe enough to repent and trust Christ. And now I understand about baptism."

Looking around at the group of sixteen and then directly into the eyes of Gordon, Mr. Miller said, "There is more to be spoken at another time. This is a good place to stop and let you boys return to your homes and think on these things. We have done well on this Lord's Day. We've had good food and good fellowship all among good friends. Perhaps next time we can talk about the anabaptists. Let us all stand for prayer."

Two weeks later, Gordon came cruising up like a state trooper on his maroon Schwinn.

"Hey, Curtis, did you read last night's *Daily Globe* about the event in this year's county fair?"

"Nope! Not yet," he said wiping polish off from the chrome fender of his Monarch. Taking off his thick dusty glasses, he began to clean them. "Why are you in such a dither, Gordon?"

Leaning his newly polished maroon bike against a maple tree, he brought over the newspaper. "Look at this," he said.

Curtis put his big spectacles back on and read.

Mt. Zion Bicycle Road Race
There will be a new event in this year's county fair
to be held on Saturday at the Ironwood fairgrounds.

> It is only open to amateurs. It will be a bicycle race. The distance is set at twelve miles.
>
> This is broken down into two laps of six miles each. The race will start at the grandstand, proceed south onto US 2. Then it will move eastward to Mt. Zion road. At this point it will proceed north up to the top of Mt. Zion and return back to the fairgrounds on the same route. The entry fee is two dollars. Registrations will be held Monday through Friday between the hours of 9:00 a.m. and noon at the fairground's office. You must bring your bicycle for an inspection.

Curtis frowned and looked up at Gordon. "Hmmm. I wonder if Luke will enter the race and test the Peugeot."

"We could all race." Gordon grinned. "We couldn't possibly lose, at least Luke wouldn't."

Curtis snapped his polishing rag getting rid of the dry residue. "I don't think Luke will be able to race. Even though he's a New Order Amish, they're still strict about this competition self-glory thing. Let's go out and talk to him."

Mr. Miller and Luke were hitching up the gelding and buggy for a trip into town. Sitting down on some old wooden barrels, Curtis and Gordon explained the upcoming bicycle race at the fairgrounds.

Mr. Miller spoke first. "Being New Order Amish doesn't change our attitude about sports, competition, and awards. It's wholesome to have clean fun, and there is value in being strong. We still hold to the belief of humility. Competition has a way of promoting pride."

"I've been wondering about my Peugeot racing bike." Luke looked up at the hayloft. "As much as I enjoyed fixing it up, I am struggling as to what to do with it. It really is not suited for our kind of riding around here. Why don't I let you use it in the race, if you like.

"Father, would you have any objection if Curtis rode it? He did have the fastest time in our last practice heat."

"That would be a fine solution for the time being," he said. "And we will give this some thought as to the future of the Peugeot."

On Monday, Curtis, Gordon, Bryce, and David stood in a long line of other boys waiting to register for the upcoming Mt. Zion bicycle race.

All registrants had to come with the bicycle they expected to race.

Suddenly someone near the front of the line swore and with those words hushed the voices of the onlookers.

"And keep your puny, grubby hands off my Raleigh." It was Herman, and with him were his two brothers. "I mean to win this here race and have that beautiful bicycle trophy to store my money in."

Curtis stared at his rival. "This could mean big trouble, guys. I wouldn't trust those three as far as I could throw the Eiffel Tower."

David stared ahead. "He's got a nice-looking three speed. It looks like his two brothers have a couple of Montgomery Ward bikes. Wait until they see what you have, Curtis."

Shortly after the commotion, up came Herman showing off his black and chrome English bike. He was a big chubby guy and walked flatfooted. When he saw Curtis with the racer, he glared at him and said, "What you got there, google eyes, a sissy bike?"

"No, siree! I have my Amish friend's bike, and it's so fast you can't see the wheels turning when it's in high gear. Are you sure you can ride a black bicycle? Isn't that an Amish color?"

"Not only that," interrupted Gordon, it's a French racer. Just look at the handlebars."

Herman jammed his front tire against that of the green and red Peugeot. "Remember that football game last year when Bessemer beat the great Ironwood Red Devils? Who made all the touchdowns for my team? I did, that's who. And who was so fast that you guys had to gang tackle me in order to keep me from scoring? My wheels are just as big as your spinach-looking contraption you call a bike. Wait and see. It will be the Carrolls from Bessemer who will gain the glory again."

"'Pride goeth before a fall,' Herman. We'll see you and your brothers on Saturday. Try playing fair for once."

At ten o'clock the day of the race, nearly fifty bicycles were lined up in front of the grandstand. Gordon was not going to race his heavy Schwinn. They had agreed he would be a scout at the halfway point, the summit of Mt. Zion near the concrete water reservoir.

David and Bryce were on both sides of Curtis waiting to give him the lead when the race began. They were in the middle of a long row of competitors. To the far right there was the usual commotion interspersed with profanity from the three Carroll brothers. Gordon was walking about on the sidelines checking out the competition.

Up he came with a report of his observations. "There's at least six three speeds here. Three are really old timers. Your competition will be from those bikes, but with your variety of gears, you can take off better and climb the hills easier. I checked out the Carrolls. The two younger brothers have wooden dowels taped to the under side of their crossbars. I'm suspicious about that. Something's up. Be careful, you guys."

Curtis looked up into the stands, and there along the railing he saw Veronica. She had been eyeing him for some time and smiled. Waving her hand, she motioned for him to come over to the railing.

"Hold my bike, Bryce. I'm going to see what brings Veronica here today."

Dressed in a yellow t-shirt like his three buddies, Curtis approached the girl from Wakefield. "What brings you here today, Veronica?"

"My brother," she replied, "he's in the race also. His name is Hilden. See him over there with the red and blue three-speed Phillips bicycle. He rides all over the place just like you. I'd appreciate it if you would keep an eye out for him. He's fourteen, but I think he has a chance of winning. Well, maybe next to you, Curtis. He's really fast and a horse on the hills."

"Hey, Veronica! I see you're in the pink today." He smiled with a glitter in his eyes. She was the one who usually had the humor. Her deep pink pleated cotton skirt with a pastel blouse matched the blush in her cheeks. A gold locket was suspended from her neck. A yellow ribbon was gathered into her long wavy brown hair with its tint of auburn.

This was only their third meeting, but his heart soared like an eagle whenever he looked at her. She had grown since the last meeting two years ago at the ski jumping meet in Wakefield. She was taller and slender, much like Leah.

Veronica smiled back. "I see you're wearing yellow, Curtis. Why is it that you wear that color? Is it because of the award I gave you at the ski jump when you won the meet?"

"I still have the yellow silk scarf," he answered.

"Guess what, Curtis. If you win this race, I have another yellow award to present to you."

The loudspeaker blared, "Five minutes to race time. Only racers on the course please."

Curtis was really motivated now. He had the best bike in the country and his friend with the yellow ribbon in her hair viewing from the grandstand.

Down the clay-covered racetrack the bicycle stampede rolled. Out the gate and out of sight they flew. The green Peugeot was in the lead closely followed by the black Raleigh and then the red Phillips.

David and Bryce had Curtis in their sights until the turn onto the road leading to Mt. Zion. They decided to follow the two younger Carroll brothers and make sure there was nothing crooked going on. Gordon would be at the top of the hill and give them a status report about Curtis, Herman, and the other three speeds. They both realized that when the ten-speed and three-speed bikes were in the highest gear, the revolutions of the cranks would be the same; consequently, the speeds would also be about identical. It was critical that Curtis maintain his lead.

At the crest of the hill near the water tower, Gordon yelled to his two friends, "Curtis has the lead by two minutes, and Herman is second. Another rider on a red three-speed is not too far behind him."

David and Bryce began their descent closely behind the two Carrolls. David yelled at Bryce, "You follow behind me as close as you can. They're taking their wooden dowels off. Something's up with those jokers."

The four bikers were flying down the hill so fast that peddling was useless. David was drafting and gaining on the Carroll brothers. Suddenly the two Carrolls separated leaving the middle open, and David shot between them, but too late to realize his fate. One of them took his dowel and jammed it into the rear wheel of David's bike. His rear tire screeched on the pavement with the smell of burnt rubber. He went into a side skid with his bare leg and peddle rubbing against the road.

Bryce shot past the scene on the far right evading David's crash and the other boy with the dowel. He slammed on his coaster brake to stop as the two Carroll brothers went sailing by croaking like chickens with their heads cut off. "We got him, Jimmy, we got him. Two to go."

Bryce helped David remove his bike off the road as other racers zipped by.

"I can't race," groaned David. "My rear wheel's shot, and my left leg is scraped up bad. I want you to keep going and keep an eye on those two culprits. I bet you they're out to get Curtis next. I'll walk back up the hill and get with Gordon."

Bryce tore off down the hill, sped down the road to the highway, and on towards the fairgrounds. The Carroll brothers on their red and white bicycles were nowhere in sight. After awhile he began to notice the riders from the first lap coming towards him. He quickly spotted the yellow jersey of Curtis still in the lead. Curtis slowed a bit as he noticed the yellow jersey of Bryce. They had all agreed to wear the same colored jerseys. That color was always worn by the Tour de France leader.

Bryce shouted ahead to Curtis. "Be on guard. The Carrolls got David's bike with a dowel rod. He's out of the race."

Curtis answered back. "That kid on the red bike is really pushing Herman. They gain on me slightly in the straightways, but I'll gain it back on the curvy hill up Mt. Zion. See you at the grandstand."

Meanwhile, David and Gordon got together at the top of Mt. Zion and came up with a plan. They reasoned that the two Carroll brothers would do anything to help Herman win.

"I think they will try to ambush Curtis at the worst spot for a racer on this course. Some place where there are no people and where it's dangerous," reasoned David.

"That would have to be the steepest long run before that big curve near the bottom," offered Gordon. "Hey! There's blood oozing from your leg again. Let me take our handkerchiefs and tie them together. At least this will bandage your gash and maybe stop the bleeding."

Not knowing whether the Carroll brothers would try to stop Curtis before or after the curve, they each positioned themselves one above and one below that location. Hiding behind the huge boulders beside the road, they waited for Curtis to appear.

Bryce had not seen the Carrolls since David's wreck. Surely he would have met them on the return lap, but they had totally disappeared.

All was quiet except for the afternoon singing of the robins, and the balmy wind coming up from Wisconsin. Both boys waited.

After leaving Bryce, Curtis made his turn onto Mt. Zion Road. He could make out five bikes behind him, but a good dozen blocks away. *Give me the hill,* he said to himself. *These gears will double my distance. What a bike.*

He began his ascent. A quarter of an hour later he crested the top and the familiar water reservoir. *Where is Gordon?* Something was wrong. *Will those goofy Carrolls win at any cost?*

He plunged into the steep curvy descent. Down, down, down — faster, faster, faster, until he could no longer out-peddle his speed. He descended like a meteor. Trees and rock escarpments went flying past. His eyes began to water with the speed and the air turbulence built up behind his thick glasses. Insects bounced off. He must be doing over forty miles an hour.

He had memorized the course and knew that on the last big sharp curve he would have to lay the bike way over nearly on its side and take it on the inside. Seconds seemed like minutes, and minutes like hours. And then he saw it——the last major curve up ahead. Leaning drastically into the left turn, he completed the dangerous arc and righted his bike. He froze on his handlebars. Across the road, two red and white bicycles setting on their kickstands blocked his path. He squeezed the hand brakes as hard as he could. In seconds the green and red Peugeot would be trash, and he might be at death's door. The bike began skidding. The smell of rubber came from his tires and brakes.

Suddenly a flash of two yellow shirts appeared running beside the road. Each grabbed the handlebars of the two red and white bikes and whirled them over the edge of the road into a rocky ravine. Curtis grinned as he fishtailed past his two friends. The bicycle blockade had vanished, and the knuckles of Curtis were as white as his face.

Now through a long gentle right-hand turn, Curtis descended onto the straight stretch before the highway. He had won. *Right is might,* he thought. *Truth and kindness are vindicated*. Luke would be happy with the results. What a story he had to tell the Millers.

A few spectators had gathered at the bottom of Mt. Zion. As Curtis entered the long straightaway, someone shouted, "If you hurry, you can catch the leader."

He responded back, "I am the leader. No one has passed me yet."

Yelling back, another onlooker said, "The big guy on a black bike is ahead of you."

Curtis strained his eyes through the smudged glasses. Sure enough, there was Herman almost to the intersection of U.S. 2. How could this have possibly happened? How did Herman Carroll get ahead of him?

Slowly, he began to realize that there were no judges at the top of the hill. The last one was positioned at the upcoming intersection. Herman must have taken that old two track in the trees near the bottom of Mt. Zion.

That was cheating. He needed a witness. He would have Gordon and Bryce, but then Herman would have his two brothers so that wouldn't work. Then he thought of Veronica's brother who was in third place and not too far behind Herman. Looking behind him, Curtis saw Hilden Lauti coming out of the last curve.

In his favor, Curtis had his bicycle training and the fact that his Peugeot was much lighter than Herman's. Both bicycles were close to the same gearing in the highest gear, but weight was important. One thing he hadn't known about was a trick Herman had picked up from his dad. If you over-inflate your tires, there will be less friction, and you will travel much faster. Herman had filled his tires with eighty pounds of air instead of sixty. On the other hand, Herman's overall weight was a handicap.

As he held the bottom curve of his handlebars to become more aerodynamic, he could see that he had gained half the distance between the two of them by the time Herman reached the intersection. He had had a tremendous run down Mt. Zion. Herman would have had a slow start. He must have waited in the woods off from the two track for a signal from his brothers.

Along the main highway, more people had assembled and began to cheer Curtis as his flushed face knifed the head wind. The gearing down would help him more than his rival. The derailleur was a Godsend.

Curtis cut the distance in half again as Herman reached the gravel road to the fairgrounds. Bryce was waiting at the corner and shouted, "He's bushed! I don't think he can make it to the stadium."

A quarter of a mile to go. He shifted down again. His legs were pumping like pistons. The neck muscles ached. His hands were numb from the long grip on the handlebars to gain leverage in the push on each peddle.

Curtis groaned, "Oh, Lord, it doesn't look good. He's at the entrance to the fairgrounds."

Herman entered the horse track from the south gate. It was furthest from the grandstand. A cheer went up. A half a lap, and he would be the winner.

Through the same gate came Curtis. Herman was halfway around. The bleachers were full of people. They rose to their feet applauding.

Then it happened. Kerpow! Over the handlebars Herman catapulted into a cloud of red iron-ore dust. His over-inflated front tire had blown. He sat up looking back at his approaching rival in the yellow shirt.

Curtis slowed down attempting to pass near the downed bike and his adversary. As he swerved to miss the black Raleigh, Herman kicked at his own bike in disgust and anger at the same time attempting to strike the Peugeot and dislodge Curtis. A shot was heard that hushed the crowd as the rear tire of Curtis exploded after striking the sharp pointed teeth of Herman's sprocket. Down he tumbled.

Herman screamed at him with his face laden with red dust and sweat. "Hey, Specs! Welcome to the club."

Both boys seemed to realize at the same time that they needed to finish the race in order to be declared the winner. Simultaneously, Curtis and Herman picked up their bicycles and began to run with them towards the referees holding the ribbon.

The crowd began to applaud the scene before them. Someone yelled, "Look, another rider!" Onto the track came the third-place rider on his deep red and blue Phillips. It was Veronica's brother, Hilden.

It was now a mad rush to the finish line. Two young men pushing their bicycles with flat tires. The face of justice against the face of hate, both wrinkled in agony from the torture of a hard twelve-mile race.

The younger boy on his three speed gained on the twosome pushing their bikes. Upon reaching them and about to pass, he abruptly jumped off his bike. To the surprise of the standing audience, Hilden Lauti began running and pushing his bike. Cheers went up. This was unreal.

In a near dead heat, Herman's right foot hit his peddle. Down he went with his bike on top of him. He profaned the scene by cursing his bike and God.

Curtis crossed through the red ribbon with Veronica's brother near his side. He had won in spite of a near tragedy and the cheating of Herman and his brothers. Hilden came over and shook his hand as other cyclists moved across the track to the finish line. It was over, but "what price glory?"

Lingering on the clover-mixed lawn near the starting exit, the four boys from Roosevelt School were together with their families, along with Veronica, Hilden, and their parents.

"Did you ever see anything like that in all your born days?" Mr. Lauti said to his wife. "There sure are many ways to win a race, and I think we saw them all today; Herman's cheating, Curtis' courage, and Hilden's sportsmanship. Wow! What a story this would make."

Mrs. Lauti came over to Curtis and shook his hand. "You sure have come a long way from that bike trip to Iron River. And my, how you've grown. Perhaps you didn't know that my husband is a Michigan state trooper, and that is why we live in Wakefield. We were transferred here about five years ago from the post in Cadillac."

Veronica came into the circle and made an announcement. "I promised Curtis that if he won today, he would receive a personal award from me for his valiant effort. Of course, his teammates had a lot to do with that."

Removing the yellow ribbon from her hair, she approached Curtis and tied it around his neck. "There," she said, "for bravery above and beyond the call of duty, I present you with the Tour de Mt. Zion yellow ribbon of victory."

As the fragrance of lilac perfume rose from the maize material, his heart melted like butter on hot biscuits.

"All...I...I...I...want to say is that I hold this silver race cup because of Luke and my best friends. And Hilden surprised us all, by letting me win. Thank you for being here for me. And the yellow ribbon, Veronica, will grace the rim of this cup in honor of your faith in me."

On Monday, Bryce's dad drove the boys with the Peugeot out to the Miller farm. After an assembly with the family rehearsing the events of Saturday, Luke and the boys installed a new tire and tube on their gem.

"Have you decided about the bike yet?" asked Curtis.

"I'm still thinking," he replied. "Father told me it was my decision."

Curtis reached into his pocket for a letter he had received from the Peugeot company in France.

"This came in the mail Saturday. I read it to the guys this morning. Perhaps it will help you in your decision.

"Well, we've got to be going. We register for our classes and get our lockers today."

"One thing before you go," spoke Mrs. Miller. "We would like to have you boys and your families come out for a summer's end dinner next Saturday. Since the new school year is about to start, we want you to join in our harvest celebration. It is a custom of ours. We will make ice cream in our dairy. We have those freshly canned strawberries, raspberries, and blue berries you helped us pick this summer. And you can have all the corn on the cob and fried chicken you can eat.

I'm also wondering, Curtis, since Hilden was an important part of the events on Saturday, could you contact his family and invite them also?"

Curtis nearly jumped out of his shoes. "Could I? Terrific! Wow! I mean Veronica, too!" He took off his glasses and wiped his eyes. "Thanks, Mrs. Miller. You too, Mr. Miller. And all of you Millers. You're all super!"

David limped over to Mrs. Miller, took her hand, and kissed it. "Mrs. Miller," he said, "you are an angel. I don't have a mother. She died years ago when I was a baby. My grandparents raise me. Thank you so much."

Curtis, Bryce, and Gordon also came over and each gave her a big hug.

Saturday came, and the boys were dressed in their various colored L. L. Bean chamois shirts and tan corduroys. They had ridden out with their bikes, and at the head of the pack, David was parading a brand new orange Raleigh three speed. His dad had just returned from duty with the Navy in England.

The food was arrayed on tables under a large maple located between the house and the tool shed. Steaming corn on the cob, fried chicken, freshly baked biscuits, churned butter, pitchers of milk, roasted German sausage, potato salad, and jams galore were inviting the crowd to eat.

Mr. Miller rang an old cowbell that Jeremiah had retrieved from the barn. "We welcome the families of Luke's newfound friends. We also thank them for lending the boys to us for part of the summer. Much farm work was done because of them. As is our custom, let us pray and thank God for our food.

"Father in heaven, we give thee praise for your providence in bringing Curtis, David, Bryce, and Gordon into our lives. And we thank you for their families. Receive our thanksgiving for the provision of safekeeping for the events of last Saturday. We all run a race called life, and it is our hope not to be disqualified because of some selfish deed. We forgive those who have acted in malice towards us. Thank you for the preparations of this food, for its abundant supply, and may it strengthen our bodies to be used for your glory. Amen."

The sky was summer blue. The air had that freshness out of the north from nearby Lake Superior. The cows were mooing, horses whinnying, and the chickens clucking. This was a farmstead at its best.

The hungers for homemade cooking had been tantalized by the aromas of food prepared by hard work and love. Voices of laughter, clinking of dishes, and words of gaiety marked this as a memory in the making.

Curtis sat across the table from Veronica and Gordon from Leah. Veronica wore a yellow dress with another yellow ribbon in her hair. Leah was dressed in a full-length lavender dress. Her hair was done up like her mother's revealing her delicate facial features. Both girls sat next to each other and shared special thoughts as sixteen year olds often do.

After everyone's fill of homemade vanilla ice cream smothered with a berry topping, tours were given of the farm to the families. The children engaged in a softball game with even little Rachel and Lydia getting a turn at bat.

By late afternoon, the gathering reassembled under the old sugar maple. Various ones spoke. There was anxious anticipation as to Luke making an announcement about his bicycle.

David's dad, dressed in his white Navy uniform, thanked the group for their friendship and kindness to David, since he was seldom able to be home.

Matthew and David thanked the four boys for teaching them so much about bicycle building.

Many others had comments of various sorts. Finally Luke, who had disappeared for a short time, entered the circle of friends pushing his recently waxed green and red Peugeot racing bike.

"It's my turn now," he said. "You have been wondering about my decision concerning the bicycle. You may not have known the contents of the letter Curtis received from France. Unknown to us, the letter stated that this Peugeot bicycle once belonged to a French racer. His name is Jacques LaSalle. He won the Tour de France in 1938.

"The Peugeot company was curious about this bicycle because it was so old. They traced the serial number to LaSalle and discovered that this was an experimental model that the company and LaSalle were developing specifically for the Tour de France. This was in the early 1930's. At that period the Tour would only permit one-speed bicycles. We knew it was only a matter of time before derailleurs would be permitted."

Luke stopped his speech and turned to Curtis. "Come up here, my friend, and read the rest of the letter. You were the one responsible for writing the Peugeot Cycles Company in the beginning of our project."

Curtis read the correspondence:

> "Mr. LaSalle was given the bicycle for all his work in testing it for the Peugeot Cycles Company.
>
> In 1937, the Tour de France sanctioned the use of derailleur gearing. Mr. LaSalle was provided bicycles by our company for competitive racing and had no use for the original prototype. He sold it to a soldier assigned to the American Embassy in Paris. The Peugeot Cycles Company has a long and rich history in the pioneering of bicycles. Since 1888, we have produced the finest quality bicycle possible. We now display our history at the exhibition hall. This bicycle that you young men restored was the

> first prototype used in developing a road bike for the Tour de France.
>
> We wish to purchase the bicycle from you for the exhibition hall. The serial number indicates that it was the one used by Mr. LaSalle in our testing runs, and we have nothing else like it. We are willing to offer you the sum of 15,000 francs ($500) plus the cost of shipping if you choose to sell it to us."

There were many exclamations of surprise as to the amount of the money.

Luke continued. "The bicycle is a winner. Curtis proved that last Saturday. Herman Carroll was disqualified, and Curtis would have won easily. And Hilden is a winner also considering what he did. We are all surrounded by new friends. Restoring the bike was an adventure I will never forget. More important was the learning and friendly times I had with Curtis, Gordon, Bryce, and David.

There is a verse in the Bible that says, '...freely you have received, freely give.' Although the reference is to receiving salvation through God's grace, the thought has struck me that this bicycle was also freely given to me. It's true we spent some money for the parts and postage, but I believe that it was returned in the learning and enjoyment we had with the bike.

It is my decision to give the bike back to the Peugeot Cycles Company.

There was silence as the thirty-two faces gazed at Luke. Then applause.

Mr. Miller came up to his son and shook his hand. "It is a good decision, my son. You are casting your bread upon the waters, and it will return unto you many times."

Gordon rose and came up to Mr. Miller. "I have something to share. Most of you know I have had a struggle with this baptism thing and understanding the difference between Christian and

Amish. Thanks to Mr. Miller and Curtis, I now see clearly what the truth is. It is not about what we hear about the Amish, or New Order Amish, or even Christian, but what the Bible says is the truth and Jesus Christ.

"Last Wednesday, I came out and talked with Mr. Miller and told him I wanted to become a follower of Christ. We both prayed in the tool shed, and I repented of my sins and believed on Jesus Christ as the Son of God. He is now my Savior and Lord. I have told this to my parents, and they have encouraged me to be baptized."

Curtis rose from the lawn and walked over to Luke, Mr. Miller, and Gordon. Tears ran like a spring rain down his face. He removed his heavy glasses revealing those passionate blue eyes. The scent of roses flowed from near the front porch where a white trellis was intertwined with yellow climbers. He stroked the green and red bicycle that he dearly loved. His own bicycle had been one of his truest friends when he had had no friends. At the age of twelve, when he picked up that beautiful blue and ivory Monarch, it had been his constant companion. And then Bryce, Gordon, and David had entered his life as new friends.

He needed courage now more than ever for what he was about to say. No one in his family was a Christian. He looked for yellow, the girl in the sunshine dress. She would give him that strange glow of trust through her eyes. He found her, and his confidence was renewed.

"When I saw those two red and white bicycles blocking the road Saturday, I realized, quick as a flash, that my life could end in a split second. The race, the winning, it was not important. If this was the Providence of God for my life, I wasn't prepared for it to end so quickly. Why did I want to race? Why did my friends race? Why does anyone race? Was it for the gold, glory, or God? Could it have been for self? Was it for my glory? Was it to build my lack of confidence because I wear thick glasses and tend to dwell on my weaknesses?

"You will never know the joy in my heart when I saw David and Gordon run out onto the road and fling those bikes off the cliff. And you will never know the disappointment when I saw that black bike of Herman's far away in front of me.

"Mr. Miller had shared with us an important truth weeks ago. 'And what shall it profit a man if he gain the whole world...?' Was I gaining something just for myself? Remember, he also quoted from the Scriptures, 'If any man will come after me (Jesus), let him deny himself and take up his cross and follow me.' You see, there it was right in front of me, clear as spring water.

"Now I understand better what Luke said about the New Order Amish. 'Engaging in sports competition for the glory of the reward is the glorification of self.'

"What I will remember most about this race and what God has taught me is that the most meaning in any activity is the relationship you have with friends. It is the sacrifice they are willing to make for the benefit of others. That is what I call love. In fact, that is what Christ said, 'Greater thing can no one do than lay down his life for others.'"

Mr. Miller said, "Amen." Luke repeated it, and then Gordon. And throughout the audience there was a chorus of "Amens."

Curtis looked at Veronica again. Her eyes were moist, and her flushed cheeks reflected a glisten from the tears that flowed down upon her lap. "My last comment is an announcement. The Lord willing, I am going into the ministry. After I graduate from high school this spring, I plan to go to North Park Seminary in Chicago. God bless you all for being my circle of friends."

In the silence was heard the tumble of cascading waters from Spring Creek as it flowed past the stone tool shed wandering on its long pathway to Lake Superior. The ricocheting water against the stones seemed to be repeating, "Gen-tle-ness is good...gen-tle-ness is good...gen-tle-ness is good."

CPSIA information can be obtained
at www.ICGtesting.com
Printed in the USA
FFOW03n0629071217
43960285-43089FF